"YOU REALLY ARE THE ULTIMATE TEASE."

"It doesn't matter if your hair is up or down, whether you're in a gown or old jeans, you make my mouth go dry with wanting you. But that's not what you want. What is it about me that turns you off so?" He turned to look at her again. "When I kissed you before I could swear you enjoyed it, but now . . ." He trailed off.

She stirred slightly, trying to make herself reach out to him. "I still feel the same way."

"Which is what? How?"

She laughed a little. "Scared. I don't know what to do."

"Let me show you. Let me love you."

"That's the first time you've used that word, Rod."

"What word? *Love?*" His grip on the steering wheel tightened. "Damn it, Alex. You want me to say I love you when I don't even know you yet."

"You want me to jump into bed with you when I don't even know you yet," she countered.

A CANDLELIGHT ECSTASY ROMANCE ®

162   VIDEO VIXEN, *Elaine Raco Chase*
163   BRIAN'S CAPTIVE, *Alexis Hill Jordan*
164   ILLUSIVE LOVER, *Jo Calloway*
165   A PASSIONATE VENTURE, *Julia Howard*
166   NO PROMISE GIVEN, *Donna Kimel Vitek*
167   BENEATH THE WILLOW TREE, *Emma Bennett*
168   CHAMPAGNE FLIGHT, *Prudence Martin*
169   INTERLUDE OF LOVE, *Beverly Sommers*
170   PROMISES IN THE NIGHT, *Jackie Black*
171   HOLD LOVE TIGHTLY, *Megan Lane*
172   ENDURING LOVE, *Tate McKenna*
173   RESTLESS WIND, *Margaret Dobson*
174   TEMPESTUOUS CHALLENGE, *Eleanor Woods*
175   TENDER TORMENT, *Harper McBride*
176   PASSIONATE DECEIVER, *Barbara Andrews*
177   QUIET WALKS THE TIGER, *Heather Graham*
178   A SUMMER'S EMBRACE, *Cathie Linz*
179   DESERT SPLENDOR, *Samantha Hughes*
180   LOST WITHOUT LOVE, *Elizabeth Raffel*
181   A TEMPTING STRANGER, *Lori Copeland*
182   DELICATE BALANCE, *Emily Elliott*
183   A NIGHT TO REMEMBER, *Shirley Hart*
184   DARK SURRENDER, *Diana Blayne*
185   TURN BACK THE DAWN, *Nell Kincaid*
186   GEMSTONE, *Bonnie Drake*
187   A TIME TO LOVE, *Jackie Black*
188   WINDSONG, *Jo Calloway*
189   LOVE'S MADNESS, *Sheila Paulos*
190   DESTINY'S TOUCH, *Dorothy Ann Bernard*
191   NO OTHER LOVE, *Alyssa Morgan*
192   THE DEDICATED MAN, *Lass Small*
193   MEMORY AND DESIRE, *Eileen Bryan*
194   A LASTING IMAGE, *Julia Howard*
195   RELUCTANT MERGER, *Alexis Hill Jordan*
196   GUARDIAN ANGEL, *Linda Randall Wisdom*
197   DESIGN FOR DESIRE, *Anna Hudson*
198   DOUBLE PLAY, *Natalie Stone*
199   SENSUOUS PERSUASION, *Eleanor Woods*
200   MIDNIGHT MEMORIES, *Emily Elliott*
201   DARING PROPOSAL, *Tate McKenna*

THE MAN WHO CAME TO STAY

Margot Prince

A CANDLELIGHT ECSTASY ROMANCE ®

Published by
Dell Publishing Co., Inc.
1 Dag Hammarskjold Plaza
New York, New York 10017

Copyright © 1984 by Marjorie Price

All rights reserved. No part of this book may be
reproduced or transmitted in any form or by any
means, electronic or mechanical, including photocopying,
recording or by any information storage
and retrieval system, without the written permission
of the Publisher, except where permitted by law.

Dell ® TM 681510, Dell Publishing Co., Inc.

Candlelight Ecstasy Romance®, 1,203,540, is a registered
trademark of
Dell Publishing Co., Inc., New York, New York.

ISBN: 0–440–15298–4

Printed in the United States of America
First printing—January 1984

To Our Readers:

We have been delighted with your enthusiastic response to Candlelight Ecstasy Romances®, and we thank you for the interest you have shown in this exciting series.

In the upcoming months we will continue to present the distinctive sensuous love stories you have come to expect only from Ecstasy. We look forward to bringing you many more books from your favorite authors and also the very finest work from new authors of contemporary romantic fiction.

As always, we are striving to present the unique, absorbing love stories that you enjoy most—books that are more than ordinary romance. Your suggestions and comments are always welcome. Please write to us at the address below.

Sincerely,

The Editors
Candlelight Romances
1 Dag Hammarskjold Plaza
New York, New York 10017

CHAPTER ONE

Alexandra Baxter looked through the French doors at the winter-blighted patio lit for the occasion by strategically placed spotlights. The lights bathed handsomely tubbed hemlocks that needed only the blessing of snow to be seasonally correct.

"It almost makes you doubt Santa Claus, doesn't it?" said a deep voice just behind her.

Surprised, Alex turned and looked up into an unfamiliar, shadowed face. She almost smiled, thinking that from what she could immediately see, Eliza and Henry had outdone themselves this time. He was well over six feet tall, lean, with broad shoulders and a handsome full moustache that wasn't droopy or affectedly curled at the ends.

"New England doesn't always have a white Christmas," she admitted, "but Concord usually tries not to disappoint. We still have a few days yet."

"Only two. After Christmas Eve it doesn't count."

She laughed and automatically started to sip from her

glass, forgetting it was empty. He took it from her. "Let me get you another."

"White wine, thank you."

As the stranger turned away, Henry Chandler came into the room from the other door. "Ah, good," he said, bustling over to Alex, "I see you two have met. I'm so glad. I'm afraid I'm a terrible host sometimes." He beamed at Alex, then said, "Rod, may I drag her away for just a few minutes?" He didn't wait for an answer, though Rod raised her wineglass in a salute of assent, but herded Alex back the way he had come.

Alex was never offended by Henry's officious meddling —he and Eliza were too dear to her—but she couldn't help smiling when, as now, they gave with one hand and took away with the other. She didn't doubt for a second that this Rod was "hers" for the evening. The pattern was clear. He was the only man at the party she didn't know; hence, he had been imported, at who knew what trouble and expense, for her. Under some other guise, of course, but one so transparent only Eliza and Henry would really believe it.

Henry shut the library doors. "Well?" he demanded. "What do you think of him?"

She was going to tease him a bit, but something in his manner stopped her. Even for optimistic Henry, who sincerely believed each man he unearthed for Alex was the answer to her maidenly prayers, his excitement was exceptional. Instead, she smiled and said judiciously, "Very presentable, Henry."

He sputtered like an overfilled teakettle. "Presentable! Oh, my dear Alex! I bring you Rod Gilbert, horse trainer *extraordinaire,* place him at your feet, and you call him presentable?"

8

In spite of herself, Alex was impressed, but she wasn't going to let Henry know—not yet anyway. She laughed. "Perhaps I would have come up with an adjective more to your liking if we'd had a chance to say more than two words to each other. We hadn't even exchanged names yet, so how could I have known he was at my feet?"

"You hadn't been introduced?"

"I suspect we'd have managed that part nicely. Maybe when he brings back my drink?"

"But he came tonight just to meet you. He's heard so much about you."

"From two little birds named Eliza and Henry?"

"The first mention, yes, but *he* actually asked *me* if I'd introduce him to 'this Alex Baxter he'd heard of.' " Henry imitated Rod's deep voice, clutching her hand as he reverted to his normal pitch. "Wait till you hear what he wants. It will be the making of your whole operation."

Alex's whole operation was seventeen acres of land, a riding school, stables for eighty horses, and a newly constructed indoor riding ring on the outskirts of Concord. At only twenty-five, last year Alex had used her patrimony to buy Sunny Meadow Farm when its owner, a vigorous horsewoman in her late sixties, fell and broke her hip. Henry had advised her throughout the purchase, remaining a steadfast ally, so when he spoke, she listened.

But she bristled inside as she heard the word *wants*. Sunny Meadow Farm was hers, lock, stock, and backbreaking mortgage. She loved and admired Henry. He knew horses as well as business, but he wasn't always right. There were times she had resisted his schemes, and been right to do so. She had also gone ahead with things he didn't approve, like the indoor ring, because without it she couldn't have her dream of a first-class riding school.

Alex gently broke away from Henry's grip and walked to another set of French doors. "What is it he wants?"

"He wants to settle here in New England, make this his base."

"In Concord?"

The excitement bubbled over again. "Not only in Concord, at Sunny Meadow Farm."

"It's not for sale." Alex snapped the words out without thinking.

"No, no, dear. He doesn't want to buy the place, just work there."

She laughed out loud. "Oh, Henry, come on, don't be absurd. You think Rod Gilbert wants to work at my little two-bit farm?"

"Well, he doesn't want to clean stalls and drive the hay wagon, love, but, yes. He wants to affiliate somewhere and operate out of that place, teaching and training jumpers."

Alex was speechless.

"I admit, Alex, I hardly believed it myself. I've known Rod, oh, seven or eight years, watched him come up as one of the great ones." He sat back on the edge of his huge walnut desk and shook his head. "He had more than a few rough edges in those early days, I can tell you."

Alex turned to look at Henry, hoping he was not going to get lost in reverie just now.

He didn't. "I'll let Rod do most of the explaining himself. He knows his motives better than I do. I just wanted to tell you, warn you, I guess, so you wouldn't be too quick to say no." He cocked his head to appraise her. "You are a bit negative, you know."

Alex bristled openly this time. "Negative? Henry, that's not true. I have a very positive approach to life."

"To life, yes, but not to suggestions made by others,

10

especially when they come at you before you've been mentally prepared. Then you say no first and think it over later. This is something I want you to think over first—a long time."

Alex took a deep breath, a thousand rebuttals clamoring for expression.

"As a favor to me," Henry said firmly. "I'm calling in all my IOUs, honey. Listen to him, think about it, *consult* with someone besides yourself."

"You, for instance?"

"For one instance, of course. But don't go just by me. Ask around. Find out about Rod. Then make your decision." He fell silent and Alex could only look at him soberly. "One thing I want you to know, Alex," he said. "Whatever anyone else tells you about Rod, take it from me, he's a good man, a man of his word, one you can trust. Not everyone will tell you that, and they'll probably have their reasons for what they say, but I know him and I trust him, even with you. And you know how I feel about you."

Alex's eyes misted over and she blinked hard to clear her vision. She reached a hand to Henry and nodded. "Okay. Thank you. I love you too."

He stood and kissed her forehead, as fatherly as he looked. "Now, may I go find him and properly introduce you two?"

"As long as you control the hyperbole. I'm not God's gift to the horse set, even in Massachusetts, and I'm a long way from being a Grecian goddess."

"You couldn't prove it by me in that dress," Henry answered fervently. "Your dear father wouldn't have let you out of your room tonight."

He was right, of course. Alex's father—Alexander, but known as Lex—had approved only of Peter Pan collars;

11

lamé halters were unthinkable. But Lex and his slightly more permissive mate, Theodora, had been dead nearly four years, so Alex had finally stopped asking herself, What would Dad think? At least about clothes.

In other matters Lex Baxter had encouraged Alex to stretch herself. She had been given a unisex upbringing, one that fostered self-reliance and a certain kind of daring. The one exception had been sex. In that, Alex lived but one step from the cloister. As an only child who attended all-girl schools and the kind of horsy summer camps only girls enjoy, she had next to no experience with males—even counting Win Burgess, which she really didn't.

Win had been her official boyfriend all through school. He went to the right schools, faraway schools, and was lazy enough to tolerate the kind of managing Alex's father considered part of his parental perogative. He was the son of an old friend from law school, acceptable and absent. While having Win in the wings had given Alex social security without struggle, what truly appalled her now was that they might have even drifted into marriage in the same apathetic way.

Alex considered Win's sudden defection from their implicit relationship last year a great blessing, second only perhaps to having Sunny Meadow Farm come on the market just when it did. But others, such as Eliza and Henry, preferred to cast her in the role of the jilted, brokenhearted but brave. She knew better, but she did wish she knew more about men younger than sixty and older than ten, the age of the boys she had taught in elementary school for two years after graduation from college.

Her forays into dating had not gone well so far, despite all that friends had done. Once past the introduction, when the car door shut with her inside next to the man of the evening, she was woefully ill-prepared. She was serious, even a little dogged. She was educated, able to talk about the world and its issues, but men didn't want that. They wanted to maul her; they wanted to talk about themselves. She didn't know how to cope with that. She could listen to their boasts, of course, but why should she when she didn't want the pawing that went with it?

She wanted to believe that somewhere there was a man who would be right for her as her father had been right for her mother and as Henry was right for Eliza. There were marriages all around her—Cassie and Gerald, for example—good marriages that enriched and sustained both partners, and she wanted one of those for herself. So, for now, she put on her gold lamé gown with the discreetly revealing (was there such a thing?) neckline and slit skirt and trundled off to parties like this, trusting, hoping, that one day she would meet someone right.

As Henry led her by the hand to meet Rod Gilbert officially, all that trust and hope left her mind. Henry had erased it with his warning in the library. Rod Gilbert might be attractive, but he was much more than that, if Henry was to be believed. He was a name in show circles, a premiere trainer whose horses won at Madison Square Garden year after year. He was sought after by rich people with expensive horses. It couldn't be true that he wanted to affiliate himself with Sunny Meadow Farm. It was preposterous.

It was also true, judging from Rod Gilbert's reaction to her name. They found him waiting by the same French doors, holding a full glass of white wine, which he surrendered with a smile.

If Henry's introduction was restrained, for him, Rod's response was not. He grinned broadly, first at Alex, then at Henry, practically licking his chops. "Well, well," he said, though who it was he was addressing was unclear. Probably himself, Alex thought. "This absolutely ices it. So you're Alex Baxter."

The totally proprietary way he looked at her made Alex grow cold with anger at the same time his appreciative, roving brown eyes were heating her face with embarrassment. She could think of nothing to say, not unusual for her with a man, but her tongue-tied condition didn't bother Rod Gilbert a bit.

"When I was up here last summer making general inquiries, the name Alex Baxter kept coming up, but no one ever mentioned that you were a woman. Then I came to Henry and said, set it up for me to meet Alex Baxter. Now, to be honest, I have to admit Henry told me your sex. He even told me you were remarkable, but I'm sure he didn't say you were gorgeous. I'm afraid I expected one of those sturdy New England horsewomen with hips like a barn door."

Alex looked for help briefly to Henry. He looked flustered, and she realized he wasn't going to be of any use. She tried to escape Rod's eyes by sipping wine and turning away. Henry, already ignored by Rod, took that as dismissal.

"Well, I'll leave you two to get acquainted. If you'd like more privacy, you both know your way to the library."

Alex turned back and almost cried out in alarm. More privacy was the last thing on earth she wanted with Rod Gilbert and his devouring eyes. She watched Henry leave with a sinking feeling. She started to take another sip of wine but didn't. She was going to need all her wits.

She turned back to Rod, who had obviously used the distraction for a more leisurely perusal of her cleavage,

14

and smiled disarmingly. "I must confess, Rod, I never ate dinner tonight. Do you suppose we could find some of the solid refreshments?"

"Good idea." He roused himself and took her elbow lightly. In the more crowded room they entered, Alex could have taken up any number of conversations, and would have, but for Rod's increasingly firm direction. By the time they were midway across the handsome Oriental carpet, their progress had taken on aspects of a forced march. They didn't pause until they reached the buffet.

Alex took a plate to serve herself from an array of chafing dishes and trays while Rod went on to the bar. When he came back he took her plate from her and added to her spare selections before he put it on the commandeered tray from the bar. He then heaped another plate with finger food and put it on the tray. At the bar he ordered another Scotch and water for himself, another glass of wine for her, and lifted the burdened tray high with one hand, waiter-fashion, while he clamped her wrist in the other hand. Short of making a scene, she could do nothing but follow and hope their odd procession to the library was less conspicuous than she feared.

Inside, he let go of her wrist and set the tray on the desk where Henry had perched, before he went back to the door, shut it firmly, and turned the ornate key in the lock. "So we won't be interrupted," he said, smiling confidently at Alex.

"Isn't that a little theatrical?"

He wiggled his eyebrows at her but looked appraisingly around the room. The desk lamp and a floor lamp provided two sources of light amid the dark decorum of walnut furniture, paneling, and book-laden shelves. The Oriental rug glowed with rich reds and blues, the only colorful note beyond an occasional brightly bound book among the austere legal tomes. A brown velvet love seat and two upholstered chairs with open wooden arms formed a conversation group that Rod rearranged by bringing the two chairs near the desk for them.

Alex sat in the offered chair but used the act of sitting to slide it back from its mate. To sit in the chair as he had placed it would have brought their knees into close proximity. He pulled his chair forward to compensate, so she turned her legs to the side to avoid the contact. He appeared not to notice these maneuvers, but reached to bring the tray closer.

Alex took her plate and looked disconsolately at the amount he'd added. "When I said I hadn't eaten dinner I didn't mean for a week."

His grin lifted the corners of his brown moustache. "I can understand your problem. I can't wait to see more of you inside that dress."

Disconcerted, Alex's mind went blank again, but since her mouth was also full of ham and cheese, comment was blessedly impossible. Maybe if she ignored him . . .

"I suppose you know that dress is exactly the color of your hair in this light. Women always know things like that, don't they?" He was drinking his Scotch, not eating, watching her with what looked like amusement.

She took a stuffed mushroom and sat back a bit. "Henry tells me you're thinking of moving to New England."

"Is that all he told you?"

"Not quite, but he said you could explain yourself."

He frowned and sighed. An odd reaction, Alex thought. "Good old Henry," he said mournfully. "He has such a touching faith in the power of words."

Alex laughed and held one of the plates out to him. "Maybe if you eat something it will come to you."

He took something without even looking at it, popped it under his moustache, and chewed. It didn't seem to help. Alex found this version of the man easier to like.

"It can't be all that hard," she encouraged him.

"How old are you, Alex?"

"Twenty-six."

"I'm thirty-two."

"So? That's hardly a hundred."

He shook his head ruefully. "Looking at you I can see it's not the years, it's the miles. Or something else. I feel a hundred years old. I feel a hundred years older than Henry, for heaven's sake."

She laughed. "Everyone's older than Henry. He's the eternal Peter Pan."

He acknowledged her truth with a smile that was half grimace. "What makes it hard to explain myself is that I really don't understand myself very well right now. I feel tired of everything, especially show biz."

"Show biz? You mean horse shows?"

"Not the shows themselves so much as all the razzmatazz that goes with it: the politics, the oneupmanship, the phonies."

"You think we don't have that?"

"You have it, of course, but in far more manageable amounts."

"And you want a vacation?"

"Not just a vacation, a real change. I want to go back to basics, the horse and the rider and the ring."

"For how long?"

"I don't know. Forever? At this moment I can't imagine ever going back."

17

"At this moment," Alex said quietly, putting her plate back on the desk. "But comes another moment, another mood, and you'll get Garden fever again. Nothing is quite like ring center at Madison, I've been told."

"Yeah, that is nice. But then you go to the Got Rocks' for the victory bash and you have to charm Lolita Got Rocks and keep the drunken Mrs. Got Rocks from falling all over you." His voice trailed off.

"You have high-class problems, Rod. I'm sure you think they *are* problems right now, but you won't get a lot of sympathy around here complaining about them."

Rod hiked one eyebrow up quizzically. "No? Then I'll have to think of something else, because I definitely want some sympathy around here."

For a second Alex wasn't sure whom he was laughing at. "Your Mrs. Got Rocks sounds like a promising source of sympathy," she said. "New England women don't give sympathy easily."

"What do they give easily?"

She thought. "Not much. Advice, maybe."

He sat back, smiling. "Wonderful. Ann Landers in tweed."

"You've got it."

"How about Ann Landers in gold . . ." he floundered, "sparkly cloth?"

"Lamé," she provided.

"What would laméd Landers advise?"

"A long trip someplace where they've never heard of horses."

"Hawaii?"

"Excellent choice. Soak up sand and sun until you're as sick of that as you are of horses."

"Would you come with me?"

18

"I'm not sick of horses."

"Neither am I. You weren't listening. I like horses. I even love horses. It's all the rest I hate."

"After enough sun you'll like the rest again."

"I don't think so." He sat forward and regarded her seriously for what seemed a long time. "I've been thinking of this for a year, planning carefully. It's not an impulse, or at least not just an impulse. Last summer I came up here five or six times, scouting a location. I think I've found it. I'm prepared to put everything in order and retire up here to a new life by March of this year, in plenty of time to get ready for a new season. I have a letter written to all my associates. The only thing I need to add to it is my new address."

Alex couldn't think of a thing to say. Rod's eyes were darker now, an intense brown that seemed to go right through her, all their easy charm gone.

"Why Concord?" she managed to ask.

"Lots of reasons." He ticked them off. "Henry. It's pretty. There's enough money here for fairly decent horses. Life-style. Alex Baxter."

"Oh, come on, Rod," she protested. "I wasn't born yesterday."

"No? Then why do you look so fresh and beautiful?"

"Because I haven't been corrupted by the big bad world." She looked at him severely over her wineglass.

"Even your eyes are gold," he said, more to himself than to her.

"All the gold I have is right here." She gestured to her dress. "I don't have any money, you know."

"You have an indoor ring. You have the location I want. You don't have to have money. I'll bring you cus-

19

tomers, more than enough. You can use the extra money," he pointed out.

"Henry has a big mouth."

"Doesn't he though?"

"And what do I do with all the customers when you get sick of the pokey hick life, and the bright lights call you away?"

"I promise you a season and I always live up to my commitments."

"So Henry says."

"May I come out tomorrow to look at the barn?"

"Even if you like it, which you won't, I'm not promising you anything. It's my barn. I've worked hard and I don't want to lose it."

"I have no intention of taking it over. I'll want a free hand in my area, that's all."

"That's all?" Alex studied his face. He was probably not really handsome, feature by feature. His nose, though straight, was a bit too wide; his jaw was too square; his skin was leathery from the sun and etched by two creases in his forehead and by laugh lines. It was hard to tell about his mouth because of the moustache, but his teeth were square and businesslike. What made it all work, what was memorable, were the eyes, snapping with life. Whether he was amused or melancholy, they carried the message. Alex found them both appealing and disconcerting.

"What happens," she began, "when your area, as you call it, conflicts with some other area, as it's bound to sooner or later?" She answered her own question. "It's been my experience that men at any level of authority expect to be the boss. I seriously doubt you're any different. In fact, I suspect you're even worse than most. You have a natural authority in your manner and you know your own importance as well as I do. But it's my barn, my money tied up there, my life's work, and I'm going to run it myself, my own way. I'm very determined about that. I may be wrong frequently, but if I am, I'm going to be the one who has to live with the consequences, so I'm going to make the decisions." Alex stopped, embarrassed not so much by her vehemence as by all the "I's," "me's," and "my's" in her statement.

"I'm the soul of deference."

Alex searched his face for signs of the mockery she suspected in those words. She didn't see any, but how would she know for sure? She didn't know him.

"Hey, Alex"—he spread his open hands guilelessly—"I'm a trainer. If you think trainers have the last word, think again. I do nothing but take orders from owners, sixty-five percent of whom are women. It's the game. You're the boss lady. Even if you're wrong, you're right."

She nodded. What he said about owners was true. Perhaps it could work. If so . . .

He saw the change in her eyes, read it correctly, and sat back. His drink was empty, but the plate of food was not. Still looking at Alex, he took a large turnover to eat. "If I go for a refill of my drink, will you disappear?"

"Probably not, unless someone else comes along."

"I could lock the door and take the key."

"I could go out the French doors. And I would."

He laughed. "Then I'll just have to take my chances. Would you like wine? Or something else?"

"No, thanks."

He walked to the door and unlocked it. He sent a grin over his shoulder as he shut it behind him.

On an impulse Alex went over and turned the key again. She leaned back on the heavy paneled door, wearing a silly

21

smile she was glad no one could see. She was just reconsidering her move when the door thumped as someone tried to open it. After a second she heard Rod laugh softly. He rapped. "Alex?"

"What's the password?"

"Gold lamé?"

She considered that.

"Sunny Meadow Farm?"

She turned the key and he stepped inside, suddenly very tall and very close. She backed away quickly, all but running back to her chair.

"I knew I should have taken the key, but in spite of that dress, you look so innocent, I didn't follow my instincts." He took the other chair. "It's always a mistake not to follow your instincts."

Even without a lot of experience with men, Alex had no trouble reading the look in his eyes. "Did you see Henry?" she asked brightly. "We're not being very good guests."

"On the contrary, we're being the best possible guests. We're not bothering anyone with our boring stories. We're amusing ourselves nicely. I'd give a lot of parties if all the guests were like us."

She stood up. "Nevertheless . . ." She said nothing more because Rod also stood, even closer than before, and sensible thought left her completely. He seemed to take up all the air she needed to breathe. It wasn't just his height making her feel small, though it did. It was more a matter of tension, of suspense. He obviously found her attractive, and since he appeared to be a man of action, she found herself on edge, wondering when he would make a move. Every time he came close, the possibility of contact was distracting. She found herself wondering how it would feel

22

to be kissed by him, to be pressed against his chest, to be wrapped in his arms.

Every time it didn't happen, her relief was as huge as her disappointment. If she was supposed to be considering working with him, she could not have that relationship muddied by an emotional involvement. Business and love were like oil and water. Fortunately, Rod seemed to understand that. His eyes were bold, but he merely touched her elbow and sighed. "I suppose you're right. Lead the way, Miss Baxter. I'll do my best."

He was a charming guest. Show biz, as he called it, had given him smoothness, and the sparkle in his eyes kept it from being offensively unctuous. He said all the right things with just the slightest touch of self-deprecation, as if he were laughing at himself, even inviting others to laugh along with him. The combination was utterly winning.

Observing them together, Eliza felt a twinge of conscience. "I do hope we've done the right thing," she murmured to Henry. "She's such an innocent."

Henry laughed. "Not too innocent to wear that dress, I notice."

"That's just what I mean," Eliza said with a frown. "If she were more aware, she'd know better. I feel as if we've fed her to a wolf."

"Rod's not half the devil he appears to be."

"He doesn't have to be. I know she needs to be shaken out of her stuffiness, but going from Win Burgess to Rod Gilbert would give any woman the bends."

"She'll be fine. Stop worrying, mother hen. You have to save some energy for your own chicks."

Eliza's eyes followed his to his son Edward. Next to him was Edward's wife, Carlotta, her face dark with unspoken resentment. Eliza sighed. "We should have pushed Alex his way more. I knew, even if you and Lex didn't, that she and Win were nothing to each other."

"Alex isn't his type."

"Carlotta is?"

"No. But a different wrong would be just as wrong."

"Well, at least I like Alex," she said pointedly.

"Can't you introduce her around? Get her to stop glaring at everyone."

"It's your turn this time, my dear. I already struck out once tonight. Use your masculine charm."

He smiled resignedly. "It only works on women over fifty."

Eliza smiled back. "Don't I wish, darling."

Just as soon as Henry pushed off toward the sullen-looking wife of his younger son, Alex and Rod replaced him at Eliza's side.

"You and Henry really shouldn't flirt like that in public," Alex scolded. "People are going to start talking about you."

Eliza's patrician face brightened. "Oh, dear. But I think we're really passé by now. With such handsome young people as you around no one gives us a second thought." She reached her hand to Rod. "Have you forgiven us for bouncing you out of your room?" She explained to Alex. "We didn't know Edward and Carlotta would be coming, along with *all* the others. We had to do the unforgivable and send an invited guest down to the inn. I don't think I'll ever get over committing such a lapse."

Rod laughed. "I've forgiven you. After all, it's much quieter at the inn."

Eliza puckered her brow. "I suppose it is. Perhaps *I'll* move there too."

"How many do you have here?" Alex asked.

"They don't stay still long enough for me to count them." She kept watching Henry. "If we'd thought when we were having so many children that they'd all go off and do the same thing, I think we'd have been more sensible. Certainly if I'd known they'd all come home for Christmas . . ." Her voice trailed off:

Alex followed her gaze. "Edward looks very handsome tonight."

"Yes, doesn't he? It's so good to see him." She gave them a broad but distracted smile. "Would you excuse me?"

When she was gone Rod said, "Edward's wife looks like a real pill."

"She doesn't look very happy, but maybe it's something temporary."

"Like gas pains?"

"You're not very sympathetic," Alex protested.

"I like the people who bump me out of my lodgings to look as if they're enjoying the place as much as I would have." He took her elbow again. "Speaking of which, I could use a lift down to the inn when you go, or did someone bring you?"

"I brought myself, and of course you can have a ride. How did you come?"

"I walked, but that mood has passed."

"You don't have a car here?"

"It's in the shop till Monday. Vintage cars like mine are under repair as often as they are on the road."

"How will you come out to the farm tomorrow?"

"I'll drive you home tonight and keep your car."

"I could come for you."

"You're not very trusting."

25

"You're right. I'll see how you drive, then I'll decide."

"Get your coat."

At the foot of the stairway Alex paused with one hand on the carved newel post, about to retrieve her evening jacket from one of the upstairs rooms, when suddenly Rod put his hands on her bare shoulders and bent to kiss her. It was over before she had time to sort out the sensations that assaulted her, but she was grateful for the solid walnut support under her hand as she hung, suspended in time and space, until he pointed to the ball of mistletoe above her. "Couldn't resist," he grinned, turning her back to the stairs with a dismissive pat on her laméd bottom.

She had no idea how to operate her feet, but fortunately long practice had taught them how to manage without incident. In the bedroom she went to the nearest chair and sat. It was a vanity stool facing a mirror surrounded by soft flattering lights. She stared stupidly at her reflection and put her hands on her shoulders where his hands had been. They still felt the same to her hands, but they weren't the same. She closed her eyes. His mouth had been warm, bristled above, firm and sure, like his hands. Just the tips of her breasts had touched his chest, hardly enough to notice the contact, yet she tingled. She opened her eyes and shook her head. Dear God. This was impossible. How could she walk downstairs and get into a car with him, much less work with him every day after March?

She got up and found her coat. Wrapped in it, she felt less vulnerable. Maybe it was just the wine. She would have to be more careful. She wasn't used to drinking at all, and she'd had, what, three or four glasses of wine, and on an empty stomach, at least to start. She bent to the mirror.

Those cow eyes would have to go. She blinked hard and screwed her face into a cross-eyed grimace.

When she left the room again, her face, at least, was serenely composed. Rod was talking to Henry by the door. Even so, she descended the wide staircase as far from the bannister as she could get. She kissed Henry and let Rod's hand on the back of her jacket direct her outside into the cold.

She handed him the keys to her car and let him tuck her into the passenger's side. "It has to warm up some before it can snow," she said, shivering as a blast of cold air from the heater hit her legs and sandaled feet. She turned off the useless heater as he adjusted the seat for his longer legs, swooping them both back practically into the rear seats. Looking over at his bulk, she suddenly wished she had bucket seats and the obstruction of gears between them, but she had expressly chosen a standard front seat to be able to fit that extra passenger into the car for trips to horse shows. The car seemed little enough anyway, but with his head nearly touching the roof it shrank further.

"It may stall out a bit at first," she warned. "Do you know where to go?"

"I've been by," he said.

Of course he would have cased the farm from the outside. It made sense. She looked at the dignified houses surrounding the Chandlers', well set back from the road, decorated with the same understated look that marked everything in Colonial Concord. Not for this town a neon Santa on the roof. The restraint of a single spotlighted wreath might have seemed dull to her when she was ten, but now she found it perfect.

Rod circled the small memorial green in the center of

town and slowed before the inn. "Would you like a night-cap?" he asked.

"Oh, no, thanks."

He went past and swung onto the road that led eventually to the farm. "Maybe you could fix me coffee at your place? So I don't drive off the road coming back?"

"You're doing very well," she said.

He veered to the wrong side of the empty road in a move that threw her first against the door, then over to him. He put his arm over her shoulder, holding her there, and with an insincere "Oops," pulled her against his side. "See? I do need some coffee."

"Maybe Miriam will be up and will take pity on you."

"Who's Miriam?"

She sighed. "Sometimes I think she's the real owner of the farm. She's supposed to cook and run the house, but I haven't dared remind her of that lately."

"No wonder you're worried about me taking over," he said.

"Easy for you to scoff. You haven't met Miriam yet."

"She lives there?"

"She has one of the wings, the one off the kitchen. Frequently one of my friends stays in the room next to hers. Ellen has multiple sclerosis and Miriam helps her in return for being allowed to win at gin rummy. Ellen isn't there now, but she spends a lot of the summer with us. She finds the place lively and she's a great example for the kids around. She gives far more than she gets from us."

"Sounds like quite a place."

"It's home." She couldn't keep the contentment out of her voice, but at the moment the feeling emanated more from the placement of his arm than from the farm.

She directed him to the long driveway, warning him to

stop in front of the main house. "Usually I park around the corner of the house, but Miriam may be asleep."

"I thought she was going to give me coffee."

"When she's asleep she lets me do simple things like that, as long as I clean up afterward." As they got to the central door a ginger-colored cat mewed to be admitted. They followed the banner of her plumed tail to the right through a small dining room with ancient linoleum, the pattern of which had been erased long ago, into a neat, if old-fashioned and probably inconvenient, kitchen. Like the dining room, which had two large tables ringed with an assortment of mismatched chairs, the kitchen had seating space for eight or ten people about a round table that had seen better days.

"Can you stand instant coffee?" Alex asked, gesturing to one chair and casting off her jacket onto another.

"There's another kind?"

"There is, but it takes a while. We make urns of coffee most days, but it doesn't taste good reheated."

She put a teakettle on the stove and reached for cups and saucers from a cupboard, her gown incongruous in the slightly shabby surroundings. She was aware that he was watching her. "I feel like Cinderella. One who made it back to the kitchen before midnight," she said, sitting.

"How many people eat here in the summer?"

"A lot," she answered fervently. "We don't pay that well, but the food is terrific. It's compensation, but it also seems to help us all work together. And we don't have everybody streaking off all day on breaks."

"Then I can see why you treat Miriam with kid gloves."

"I wasn't going to do it last year. Partly I felt sorry for Miriam, but it also seemed somewhat out-of-place. I don't think any other farm operates this way anymore. Miriam

29

was so mad at me when I broached the subject, I thought I'd have to drop it anyway because she would leave. You see, she was here first; that's why I say she seems like the real owner. She ran the place for Emma Brody. Emma wanted Miriam to retire with her down on the Cape. No way. She wasn't ready to be put out to pasture yet. So she stays on in her room. Thank God."

"How old is she?"

"I wouldn't dare ask."

The cat finished eating just as the kettle started to steam. Alex jumped to the stove to remove it before it whistled. She brought it and the instant coffee to the table. "Would you let her out again? Then go into the living room to the left of the door and I'll bring the coffee."

He followed her directions and was waiting on the couch when she carried in the tray.

"When you come tomorrow, plan to join us for lunch so you can meet everyone who counts around here."

"Where do you live?" he asked, looking around.

Alex gestured to the ceiling with her head, indicating a door behind him with her hand. "Upstairs. That's a guest wing. Two rooms and bath. It's not too bad if you're into mismatched furniture. That's kind of our style here."

"You should see my apartment."

She narrowed her eyes speculatively and leaned her head against the high-backed couch. "I would expect you to have chrome and glass and plastic," she paused, "with a water bed."

He hooted derisively. "I get seasick."

"Too bad. That's my dream. I lived in a house like Henry's, only smaller, so that we called the library the den. Now I have all this splendor."

"I used to live in a van I took to shows, then I moved

up to motels on the circuit. Sometimes I think the van was better."

Alex looked around complacently. "I know this is better."

Rod put down his coffee and settled back to look at Alex. "I envy you. You're young to have put all this together."

"The price was much too dear," she said soberly. "My parents were killed in an automobile accident coming home from Florida three and a half years ago. This is what they left me."

"They owned this?"

"No. I put everything left to me into buying this. I sold the house in Lincoln, the next town over, cashed in everything I could get my hands on, and persuaded a bank or two to finance me."

"Still, you have it."

"So far." She smiled. "You can understand why I'm cautious."

"I can." He gestured with his head to the door behind them. "How about I rent the rooms behind you after March?"

She closed her eyes for a few seconds. "I'll think about it."

"I'd like to see them tomorrow. What time shall I come?"

"Whenever you'd like. Lunch is around twelve, promptly after Miriam rings the dinner bell."

"I won't be late," he promised, getting up. She started to rise. "Don't get up." He bent to kiss her forehead. "Thanks for the ride."

Alex stayed seated until the car was gone, then she went slowly up the stairs, undoing the heavy coil of hair she had

31

woven and pinned into a chignon. The hair did look almost the color of her gown as it rested on one shoulder, but it wasn't gold really, more like honey, too brown to be what she called gold. And her eyes were brown, not gold, she told herself firmly.

Nevertheless she was pleased with the evening, especially with Rod here at the house. He hadn't been put off by the run-down furniture, as many would have been. Perhaps it would work. But she'd have to stay away from wine for the duration. Brotherly kisses on the forehead were fine, but she could ill afford the emotional turmoil of the other kind. She took off the gown and hung it away. She'd give up sexy clothes too, she decided, shrugging into a flannel granny gown. Tomorrow she'd be back to jeans and her favorite perfume, essence of horse. That would certainly take care of any romance.

Alex was checking a limping horse with Cassie the next morning when Steve yelled down the stairs, "Alex, a guy here to see you."

"Send him down here, please," she called back, going on with her probing of the horse's leg. She saw his boots first and, without preliminaries, said, "See what you think of this swelling."

Rod knelt in her place as she stood. She ignored Cassie's inquiring looks, waiting quietly.

After carefully feeling the swollen leg area, Rod stood too. "I doubt very much the tendon is involved. It feels like a blow on the cannon."

"You think so?"

"Feel the edges of the swelling," he directed.

Alex felt again. "Oh, yeah. Then a soak will do it, you think?"

"It should."

Cassie could contain herself no longer. "Are you a vet?"

"Trainer," he answered, still looking at the horse's leg. "Nice horse," he said, rubbing down the horse's neck.

Alex took pity on Cassie. "Cassie, this is Rod Gilbert; Cassie Wentworth. Cassie runs the barn," she said to Rod as he reached to shake her hand.

Alex could see the wheels beginning to turn behind Cassie's button-blue eyes, so she said, "Cassie, get this leg soaking, will you? I'm going to show Rod around now. See you at lunch." Cassie's glare told her she would hear about this later, but she led Rod away back up the narrow, worn stairs.

"About twenty horses are out now on a trail ride," she said as they entered the main barn, where two horses were being groomed, restrained by cross-ties. She led him past several box stalls, from which the occasional curious horse poked its head, to stop before one door. "This is our best jumper, Freight Train," she said with a smile, "although I really shouldn't say that out loud. He's cocky enough as it is."

She watched with approval the easy way he approached the animal. At seventeen hands, F.T., as the kids called him, was the largest horse they had, discounting the pair of Clydesdales used to pull the hay wagon for public rides. A calm and sure Appaloosa who loved to jump, F.T. accepted Rod's homage as no more than his due and returned to his hay, effectively dismissing them.

By unspoken agreement they walked to the passageway leading to the indoor ring. Although Alex knew the ring was the best she'd ever seen and was well known in the area, she knew Rod would have come across better. She was nervous, aware that this was the test she had to pass if she wanted him to work there. And although she wasn't sure she ought to want him to, she already did. Above all, she didn't want to be the one rejected as not good enough. His ego would never be damaged by her; his place in the world was entirely secure. But she would be shattered if he found fault with her facility.

He didn't. As soon as they reached the ring she could tell he was pleased. He wasn't one to gush, but his eyes took it all in before he gave her an approving smile. "You did it right."

She let her breath out slowly and nodded.

"How many horses could I bring here?"

She thought. "Twenty? Maybe a few more, depending on what I can turn over in the next month or so."

"Good." He walked into the ring and looked into the rafters. "Can I see the lights?"

She went to the switch box, watching as he turned slowly, checking the way the lights faced for the badly placed spot that could temporarily blind a horse. Again he nodded and came back as she extinguished them.

"Now it's up to you," he said. "I'm more than satisfied."

She didn't take up the cue, but rather turned back to the passageway. Their boots made no noise on the sawdust footing, so the only sound as they walked was the rustling of their down parkas, played against distant neighs and whinnies. When they came to the main barn, a female voice bellowed, "Phone call for Alex!"

"Why don't you look around by yourself till lunch. Feel free to go anywhere, ask anybody anything, okay?" She ran to the front of the barn, her one long braid bouncing, and from there headed for the house. She avoided a determined-looking Cassie, who bore down on her, by looking equally determined and yelling, "I'm on the phone with someone."

"Yeah? Then you need a longer cord!"

"At the house. When I pick up there, hang up here, okay?"

She made short work of the call and escaped upstairs to her rooms. Besides her bedroom with the curly-maple four poster, she had a living room the same size as the one downstairs. But this time she didn't go there to the comfort of her parents' antique and vintage furniture, but to her office-dressing room, straight to her desk.

Once there, however, Alex merely sat in her father's chair. She didn't need to consult the books. The disheartening figures were engraved on her brain. She had to gather her courage and tell Rod he could come—not only that he could come but that he was needed. He was an outright gift of the gods. She hadn't hesitated when Sunny Meadow Farm had become available for purchase. Why act so recalcitrant now that fate had provided a boost to help her get some much needed payback on the investment of the indoor ring?

If he were twenty years older and ugly, she would jump at this chance. All she had to do was maintain a professional stance and insist on the same from him. Simple.

She got up and went slowly down the stairs. She refused to succumb to the temptation of trying to spruce up the rooms he would use. She'd checked them this morning. They were only a little better than depressing, but so what? She had warned him. She reclaimed her parka from the foot of the stairs and went outside. Rod was watching two young riders in the outdoor ring to the left of the house, but she went the other way to exchange greetings

35

with the parents of one of her pupils. When the dinner bell rang she excused herself and went to meet Rod.

He answered the question in her eyes by saying, "I like it here."

Could she do less for him? "Good, because we can certainly use you here."

"Is that yes? I mean, as long as Miriam approves?"

Alex laughed. "Better than that I can't offer by myself. Yes."

Laughing together, they filed into the dining room.

CHAPTER TWO

Early March brought delivery of two trunks to Sunny Meadow Farm, a sort of deposit that promised Rod Gilbert's ultimate appearance, but it was nearly April before he arrived in person with his four-horse van. Two of the horses were his own; the other two were harbingers of the future—horses in his charge, owned by others.

The stampede was on, and by the end of April they were turning away people and horses. Local riders who had never darkened the doors of Sunny Meadow Farm now vied for space in Rod's two classes, and some who couldn't get in were not too proud to sit on the fence and watch.

Alex would have watched along with the others except that there was too much work to be done. She had been cautious about adding staff and now faced near mutiny among the regulars, who were sorely in need of relief. Getting good, experienced workers was always a problem, and the new horses were too valuable to be entrusted to any other kind of help. So Alex often did triple duty,

37

especially during Rod's lessons, when all the crew conspired to have pressing jobs to perform within earshot of his class.

At the house Rod was king lion among a pride of females. Miriam doted on him from the moment she saw him, making Alex appear to be a liar of the most petty kind. He could do no wrong. Miriam happily picked up after him; even Ellen wheeled around in his wake trying to think of ways to please him. He was charming, distributing smiles, jokes, and blatant leers generously and impartially. Dignified dowagers fawned over him and the nine-to-fourteen-year-olds Alex taught followed him like pigeons after a popcorn-eater in the park.

But what was almost worse for Alex than the overwork and the loss of stature as most important person at the farm was the fact that all her cautious professionalism with Rod was apparently completely unnecessary. He teased and ogled her precisely as he did Miriam, Ellen, and Cassie—no more, no less. Like the sun that shines on the good and the bad, Rod smiled on females of all sorts and conditions. She did not doubt he would have kissed Miriam under the mistletoe exactly as he had her, and with the same effect. As she watched the widening swath of his influence over the females around him, she could only be thankful she had never let him see that she had been his first conquest. Nevertheless, each day she fortified her resistance, telling herself she had to continue to set the businesslike tone for their relationship, reminding herself fiercely that love and business don't mix.

The evenings Rod spent at the farm he played savage games of gin rummy, something Alex had previously thought only two could play, with Ellen and Miriam. But he was not often at home, for creamy vellum invitations addressed to Rodney Gilbert clogged the mail the way unpayable grain bills once had. Cassie breathlessly followed his romantic adventures and could not be prevented from relaying to Alex every scrap of information she procured. Her sources were amazingly accurate, to judge from the way the privileged young women showed up at the farm for private lessons, to follow up on their advantage after being escorted by Rod to one or another of the dinners given in his honor by hopeful mothers.

Nevertheless, Alex was both surprised and outraged on one of the first fine evenings in June alone on the porch off Miriam's room when Rod pushed through the screen door and dumped a string of pearls in her lap.

"Are these things real, do you know? How can you tell?" he demanded.

"I don't know." She held them to the light, turning them, then putting them against her face. "They're not plastic. Why? Where did you get them?"

"I found them in the car just now."

Alex smiled acidly. "A souvenir?"

"That stupid Celia Hewitt probably left them there." His scowl tried to join his thick rusty-brown eyebrows together over his nose.

"My, my."

"Amusing as hell, isn't it." He glared outside at his car, either blaming it for his problem or eager to be off. "I could start a boutique with the stuff women leave behind 'by accident' so they can have an excuse to 'drop by' and claim it. I usually just leave things where they lay. But if this thing is worth a lot of money, I'll be damned if I'll be responsible for it."

"High-class problems," she reminded him.

He glared at her then. "Call Hewitt for me and see if it belongs to her, will you?"

Alex threw the necklace at him. "No way! You clean up your own messes."

"It's not my mess."

"No? Well, it's sure not mine."

Rod shifted his weight from one boot to the other, finally sitting down on the other end of the couch. "Look, Alex, as a favor, please. You can say I asked you. Just this once. I don't want Celia Hewitt on my tail all summer, and if I call, she'll think it's encouragement."

"Then wait for her to call. Give them to Miriam. She'll guard you from Celia."

"You think it's funny."

"Isn't it?"

"No. Damn it, Alex, I'm just trying to get along here, and already I'm going out of my mind."

"Show biz comes to Concord. I told you we had the same things."

"You don't have to act so smug."

"Why not? I'm quite sure if you really wanted to discourage such unwelcome advances as Celia's, you'd find a way." She looked at him severely. "Crocodile tears, if I ever saw them."

He shook his head, puzzled, then he brightened. "I've got it. The best way to get rid of all of them is to have a real girl friend. If I have one girl friend, the rest will back off." He was thinking out loud. As his eyes fell on Alex speculatively she angrily got to her feet.

"Don't you say another word."

"Come on, Alex. I like you better than anyone I've met here. We could have a good time. It wouldn't mean anything."

40

She was so angry, she couldn't think of a word to say. Just when she was about to storm off the porch to get away from him, she remembered, childishly, she had been there first. She was not going to let him run her off her own porch.

So she sat down instead and took a deep breath, summoning just the right words. He took that for a change of mind and smiled broadly.

"That's better," he soothed her. "But I have to admit you really look terrific with your eyes flashing, doing those deep-breathing exercises."

"Get off this porch now." She gave him her deadliest voice and look.

"Aw, come on, Alex. Now what?"

"Don't say another word. Just go."

He said another word, his disgust turning it into a curse. "Women!" He slammed the screen door and jumped into his car, gunning the motor as he drove away.

Alex sat on the porch a long time, blank with fury. When she finally got to her feet, confettilike pieces of paper that had been a horse-show class list fell to the floor around her feet.

By the next day it was obvious Rod had found the position of official girl friend easy to fill. Robin Rhodes had been only too happy to sit on the fence during that evening's lesson, holding his jacket and dangling the keys to his ancient MG with the precise possessive assurance guaranteed to send all the other hopefuls home gnashing their teeth in frustration.

Although Alex had not been spared full view of the byplay, Cassie also had to tell her, in excruciating detail, every move Robin and Rod made. No one, Alex thought, listening with jaws that ached from being clenched could

41

wring more significance out of observed social intercourse than Cassie. Every nuance of Robin's posture, every flounce of her expensively coiffed blond hair, presented opportunities for Cassie's in-depth analysis. Just when Alex was sure she would scream if she heard one more word, Cassie's penetrating blue eyes focused on her. "You're jealous," she said quietly.

"Ha!" Alex swung around to confront Cassie. "Did it ever occur to you during the hours you've spent analyzing the Robin and Rod Show that he's just using her as a smokescreen to keep the rest of the women away?"

Cassie narrowed her eyes. "What makes you think so?"

"I don't think so. I *know* so," Alex asserted, unable to stop herself, "because I was offered the job first!"

Cassie punched that information into her circuits, then said with great sadness, "And you turned it down?" She shook her head. "You really are stupid, you know that? I love you dearly, but you don't know *beans* about men."

"I know enough to know when I've been insulted."

"I don't see Robin Rhodes shriveling up with humiliation."

Alex had to laugh, remembering his awkwardness. "Perhaps by the time he got to her he'd found another way to phrase the question."

"What did he say to you?"

"He wasn't really talking to me at first. He gave me this big sob story about girls leaving stuff in his car, chasing him relentlessly . . ."

"It's not a sob story. Have you ever seen inside his car some days?"

"I don't go peeking around . . ."

Cassie giggled. "You ought to. You'd learn a lot. These girls know every trick in the book."

Alex withered her with an icy stare. "Anyway, he just sort of came up with the idea of a front, an official girl friend to scare the others away, and his eyes fell on me because I was there. Honestly, you could just see the wheels turning in his head."

"So you got mad."

"Of course. He even had the gall to promise me it wouldn't mean anything."

"Well, you're so touchy about him."

"What do you mean, touchy."

"I don't know. You always look mad when he's around."

"I do not."

"Sure you do. Like you don't want him within five feet of you." Cassie waved aside any possible objection. "I don't mean just today. You've had No Trespassing signs up ever since he came here."

Alex opened her mouth to explain, then thought better of it. She'd already said entirely too much.

"It's because you're attracted to him, isn't it? You're afraid."

"You read too many books."

Cassie wasn't insulted; she was mentally circling her theory, ready to move in for the kill. "Of course, playing hard-to-get isn't such a bad move with Rod," she decided. "It certainly makes you stand out from the crowd around here. The problem is, you've been doing it too well. He's not terribly subtle about women."

Alex hooted with laughter.

"Oh, Alex, give the poor guy a break. He absolutely has to beat them off with a stick. How could he be expected to develop any instincts? He probably thinks you really dislike him, or something like that. Listen to your old

43

Aunt Cassie and try to loosen up a little. He's a great catch."

Alex was offended again. "If you like sharks," she retorted, happy to think of a way to end what had turned into a torturous conversation.

Cassie grinned. "The shark and the barricuda. Well, maybe you're right. Robin will at least know how to get the most out of her opportunity. It'll be interesting to see what she pulls to keep his interest. At least she has the chance to work on him, unlike some other people I could mention."

"If you say one word to anyone, if you so much as *hint* to anyone . . ."

"Really, Alex. What do you think this is? Third grade?"

"That's exactly what it is to you. But it's my life and my farm . . ."

"Yeah, yeah. You and your farm. I hope you're very happy together." Cassie turned and walked away from the fence, leaving Alex no choice but to stay on until Cassie got in her car and drove away.

Without Cassie to argue with, Alex found herself accepting some of what she had said. She hadn't realized she'd appeared to dislike Rod. Maybe she could moderate her stance toward him a bit. She wanted to be businesslike, not antagonistic. That wouldn't even do the farm any good. She was still not sorry she turned down his unspoken proposal. After all, she'd never have provided what he was getting from Robin. She didn't even know how to present such a carefully modulated show of ownership. He'd certainly chosen wisely with Robin—as long as he didn't get carried away by her.

Alex frowned, annoyed with herself for getting drawn into Cassie's way of thinking. She was being as proprietary as Robin, and on what basis? I saw him first? More third grade stuff.

She turned away from the fence, shoving the wheelbarrow ahead of her along the rutted path without looking up until she saw boots. Rod was blocking her way. She put down the wheelbarrow and tried a smile.

"Rod. I was just thinking about you."

"I could tell that from your frown," he said.

Was his touch of belligerence a defense against her supposed dislike? She let her smile grow a bit. "I always frown when I think. It's hard work for me." She rubbed the small of her back, arching slightly and unconsciously, trying to think how to phrase the idea she'd just conceived.

"Remind me to give you a back-rub after supper," he said. "I know a great way to loosen up those wheelbarrow muscles."

Stunned, Alex took her hand from her back as if she had been caught in a lewd pose. It was then she remembered she wasn't wearing a bra under her gingham shirt. The morning had been cold, but as the day warmed she had taken off both the jeans jacket and the sweat shirt that had originally protectively swaddled her figure. He smiled, apparently oblivious to her discomfort, and she could only hope he couldn't tell just how ill at ease she felt.

"I came down here to apologize for what I almost asked you the other evening. It was highly inappropriate," he said, serious again.

She had never expected an apology, but the conversation with Cassie had helped her regain her sense of humor about the incident. Accepting the apology was easy. "I should have taken you up on it," she laughed. "It might have been fun to confound the natives a bit, but I see you've solved the problem nicely."

It was his turn to frown. Alex didn't understand just what had transpired between them, but suddenly she felt much better, though she suspected Rod felt worse. What did that mean? Did she feel comfortable with him only when he acted unsure of himself? Why was he frowning now? Over Robin, or over something she just said?

"What I was thinking about just now," she began, stretching the truth a bit, "was asking if you'd go out to Northfield and possibly to North Adams to look at some stock with me. I have a buyer for two horses and I'd split my commission with you for your advice. If you haven't been out in that part of Massachusetts, it would be a nice trip. You've hardly had a minute away from here."

"Any special time?"

"It will take pretty much all day because it's two hours or so to Northfield, more to North Adams. I can arrange it around your schedule."

"Off-hand, Thursday looks good, but let me get back to you. I'd like to go. Thanks for asking." He reached to take the wheelbarrow from her, but she waved him off and returned to the barn feeling better than she had in weeks.

When Thursday dawned fresh and fair Alex could hardly believe her luck. She hurried to dress, then sat flipping blankly through an old copy of *Equus* in her living room rather than join the rest at breakfast until it was time to go. She heard Rod laugh, heard Cassie arrive, and still she sat. To go downstairs would be to expose herself to the scrutiny of too many knowing eyes. Cassie would take in every detail of her hairdo, a medium-complicated chignon; of her makeup, the natural look that takes hours to achieve; and of her clothing, crisp rust pants and jacket with an eggshell short-sleeved sweater kept from plainness by a pointillé pattern of almost peekaboo openness down the front. She wore a bra, but it was just a whisper of skin-colored nylon.

Just when she had determined that she could put off going downstairs no longer, Rod yelled from the bottom of the stairs, "Come on, Alex. Let's get this show on the road."

She looked once more into the mirror, checked her teeth for lipstick, and called, "Coming."

She really did look fine—well-dressed but casual. She squinted and contorted her features to get rid of the look of terror in her eyes, and hurried to the stairs. She made herself a blur, waving a quick good-bye to Cassie and Ellen in the dining room, and followed Rod to his car. She knew they were being watched from the window, but she climbed into the MG as if she did this every day.

Rod gave her an intense perusal as he turned the ignition, his warm brown eyes sparkling. "Very nice," he pronounced, smiling.

"You look nice too," she said. He did. He had tossed a blazer into the back seat to wear later over his chinos and neat plaid sport shirt. For now he wore a brown Shetland crewneck sweater against the cool morning air.

"It's kind of nice to wear something besides jeans and breeches," Alex remarked.

"I guess so, for a girl."

"But you'd rather not?"

"Thinking about clothes depresses me. I never get things cleaned in time and I hate to spend money on new ones."

47

"I know what you mean. I used to teach school and I had to work at keeping it all together—"

"A schoolteacher," he interrupted. "So that's it."

"That's what?" She looked at him sharply.

"That air about you."

She wasn't sure she wanted to hear what would follow, but she had to pursue it anyway. "What air?"

"Faintly disapproving, self-controlled. I should have recognized it right away. Teachers always used to think so highly of me." He threw her a withering look. "I bet you used to teach English."

"Fourth grade," she corrected him, glad to have something sensible to say. "You didn't like school?"

"Can you imagine me in school? Sitting still all day? Raising my hand to ask to go to the john?"

She laughed. "I had a lot of boys like that. It's hard for them, but schools are a lot more understanding now than when we went to school. I actually liked those kind of little boys. They just needed to move around a lot." She could imagine his restlessly physical body shrunk to ten-year-old skinniness.

"Then maybe I should have had you in school instead of the hags I had."

They swung onto Route 2 and Rod accelerated smoothly to surpass the prevailing highway speed. She sat up, trying to adjust to the uneasy sensation of being so low to the ground in a speeding sports car. He noticed her discomfort. "Relax. You'll get used to it after a few minutes."

"How fast are you going?"

"None of your business," he said evenly.

"Fifty-five is the limit." She couldn't keep from saying it, even as she knew it would have no effect on him.

He laughed. She put one bent leg under her in the

bucket seat, hitching up to see the speedometer. It was at sixty-two, not as bad as she had feared. He was aware of what she had done and drove a little faster.

She forced herself to look relaxed, laughing. "I guess I can't deny you the fun of scaring the pants off a schoolteacher."

He slowed a bit. "I don't know that I want to *scare* your pants off," he drawled, watching her. When her face flushed hotly she turned to the side window as if she were going to look at the scenery. She heard his soft laugh and closed her eyes to block the blurred view of the world rushing by outside the car. When she knew she wasn't blushing anymore she faced forward, determined never to give him such an opening again. At this rate it was going to be a long day.

She was wary and on edge, but she knew the longer she kept silent the more significance she was bestowing on what was undoubtedly with him an automatic response. Other women laughed off those remarks. If she couldn't do that, at least she could change the subject.

"How do you like it so far in Concord?" Concord seemed a less personal designation than Sunny Meadow Farm. To ask that would be like saying How do you like my only child?

"I like the farm a lot," he said, going to the heart of her question. "I wasn't wrong about what it would be like."

"And you don't miss all the advantages you had?"

"Honestly?"

She held her breath. "Honestly."

"Only once in a while. What I miss most is being anonymous. In New York I'm a cipher. In Concord everything I do is noticed."

"It's a small town."

"I was warned."

"Are you thinking of leaving?"

He laughed. "No, Alex, I'm not thinking of leaving." He let that sink in. "It would help a lot if you could relax a little."

She looked down at herself. "But I am."

"I don't mean now, or at least not primarily. The best part of being in Concord is living at the farm. I like the people and they make me feel at home. Mostly."

"But I don't, you mean."

"You tell me. God knows I'm no expert on women, but I really can't figure you. I knew you were worried about me taking over, but I thought you'd get over that."

"I have, mostly," she admitted.

"Then what is it? I've seen skittish fillies by the dozens, but you take the cake."

"I'm afraid you'll leave." It wasn't the whole truth, but it was the only part of it she was prepared to talk about.

"I've told you I won't. Am I a liar?"

"I don't know."

He glared at her, so she tried to amend that. "I don't mean that the way it sounds. I'm sure you mean it now, but I'm not sure you won't change your mind."

"That's not very flattering, Alex."

"I'm sorry. I don't mean to insult you. I just can't conceive of a man with your opportunities remaining in self-exile. The pull of what you had must be enormous."

He shook his head but didn't try to explain it all again. After a few more miles he looked at her speculatively. "Maybe you can't trust me because your parents died on you suddenly."

"Rod, for heaven's sake, don't be ridiculous."

"No," he said, suddenly seized by another idea. "I've got it. It's because of that guy you were going to marry."

Alex began to laugh. "Oh, God, not you too. I suppose you've been fed a big story about my great disappointment."

"Isn't it true?"

"I'm sorry to poke holes in your theory, but no, it's not true in the sense you mean. Win and I never had anything going except two sets of matchmaking parents. He was my designated boyfriend for more years than was good for either of us, but there was nothing behind it. The only thing his defection did was throw me to the mercies of matchmaking friends."

"That's not the way I heard it."

"No, I'm sure it isn't, but it's the truth. Eliza and Henry's version is pure invention to keep me from looking like a jerk who doesn't know how to attract men. If they call me tragically heartbroken, then my social failure is explained. It even looks like triumph upside down." Again, she had said too much, but it was a relief to confront the issue.

"What makes you think you don't attract men?"

She glared at him.

"I mean it. You've got a mirror. You're beautiful."

"I'm sure you've been too busy fighting off your own admirers to notice my lack of them."

"I assumed you were turning them down."

She laughed uncomfortably. "Honestly, Rod."

"Well, I knew the women giving me the rush in the cause of their daughters wouldn't invite you to their little bashes. After all, why make it easier for the competition? I've already got a picture of you in the gold gown firmly

51

fixed in my mind. They don't want you outshining their charges."

Her face began to redden again. "They know exactly how much they have to fear from me. They're not losing any sleep over it."

"Then they're stupid." He laughed shortly. "Which I already knew."

Alex kept her eyes on the road ahead, but she knew every time he looked at her.

"Was that Win guy the only one you ever dated?"

"Can we talk about something else, please? I've had about all of this I can take."

He took in her furious expression and laughed. "Okay. But we'll be back to the subject again. I'm very persistent."

"Then let's talk about your love life—a much more fertile field, from all I've heard."

He groaned. "Let's talk about horses. What are you looking for today?"

She told him, filing away his comments for future reference. "How did you get involved with showing horses?" she asked.

"Not the way you did, I'm sure," he said. "I dropped out of school at sixteen, actually earlier than that for all practical purposes, and got a job at a stable. I sort of had a knack for getting along with horses, better than with people, and it just developed."

"But you get along so well with people," she protested.

"I learned, but it was a hellishly bumpy road for a long time."

"How did you meet Henry?"

"He was on some committee I had to deal with." He

laughed. "Actually, it was the board that was going to suspend me; he was about the only one on my side."

"Were you suspended?"

"Not that time; later, yes."

"What for?"

"For not shutting up and being a gentleman."

"Henry said you used to have some rough edges."

"Tactful Henry. I'd have had less trouble if being a gentleman meant following his example. He was always fair."

"That's too rare in any field."

"Unfortunately, you're right." His laugh had a bitter sound. "As my horses won more often, I became more acceptable, even with my rough edges. That's also the way it is."

"From what you told me at Henry's about life with the Got Rocks I'm sure you aren't surprised by your reception in Concord. I mean with girls."

A certain wistfulness she was hardly aware of in her voice made him look over at her. "I should say no to keep up my image with you, but actually I'm more than a little surprised. Not so much to get attention, but that it's so intense. Show biz is a little bit cool, you know? They may mean it just as much under the surface, but they try not to show their eagerness. That makes it easier to pretend it doesn't matter when you refuse them."

"Do you always refuse?"

He didn't answer for so long, Alex decided he hadn't heard. Then he sighed. "I didn't, but now I will."

She turned to look at him. His jaw was squared angrily. She had hit a nerve. Part of her, the curious part, wanted to follow up with questions, but her more humane side voted to let it go.

When she said nothing more, he glanced over. "I can't believe you're going to let that go by. Especially after the way I just grilled you."

"The circumstances are obviously different. My feelings weren't involved."

"I didn't get that impression," he laughed.

"Well, not in the same way."

"How do you know? I haven't told you anything."

"You look hurt or mad; I can't tell which. I welcomed the chance to set you straight. Everyone here just talks around me, but they never ask me how I feel. I wasn't either hurt or mad."

"I guess you hit it pretty well, if you meant my pride was hurt and that made me mad."

"Then you *are* in retreat from the big-time. Personally, not professionally."

"I suppose it looks that way. Actually, the plan for retreat came first. I'm just carrying it out differently from how I had planned."

"Explain. If you care to."

"Over a long time there was one girl I was thrown together with a lot, Diana Dunbar. I trained a bunch of horses for her father and she rode some of them for quite a while. She's good, a damn good rider, and she was pretty serious about it. I certainly didn't seek her out, but as I said, we were together a lot."

"And one thing led to another," Alex supplied.

"The voice of experience?"

"Hardly. But Cassie's not the only one who reads books."

"I've thought about it a lot since last summer, and I've figured the whole thing out. We drifted into an unspoken relationship that I accepted at face value, based on her

54

background. She was the kind of girl who would get married eventually and I assumed, since she'd chosen me so aggressively, that I'd be the one she married. I knew there was a social and economic gulf between us, but I really didn't pay much attention to that. Maybe by then I'd begun to believe my own publicity. Who knows?"

"You loved her?" Alex asked.

"I didn't really think about that."

"No?" She gave him her severe look.

"That sounds like self-protection after the fact, I know, but I really didn't think much about loving her. There were so many times I didn't even like her, for Pete's sake, but there was sex, so I assumed it was the same thing. I was ready to settle down. She was there and I thought she was at the same place I was."

"But she wasn't?"

"No, I was right about that. She was out of school and we'd had a year of knocking around the country together doing the circuit. She was ready to settle down, too, just not with me."

"Someone else?"

"Not specifically. At least not right then. It was the social and economic difference."

Alex felt sorry for him. If she hadn't wanted to know so badly, she would have tried to stop him from talking.

"As I said, I've thought a lot about this and I've decided that to her I was like a year bumming around the country or working for the Peace Corps. She got to live dangerously, for her, with the option that she could bail out at any time."

He grew silent, then went on. "I could sense her restlessness. Hell, it wasn't hard. She wasn't easy to get along with on the best days. So I stepped up my retirement plans

55

and came up here to New England looking for a place to live, thinking to present her with the whole picture, marriage and a new life in the country."

"Did you?"

"No. I never got the chance. When I came back she'd moved out, back with her parents."

"Wow."

"I went after her, thinking it was just one of her games. If I hadn't been so set on seeing myself settled into a wonderful new life, I never would have been so blind." He shook his head. "She opened my eyes in a hurry."

"But you never told her?"

"No. Thank God."

"What did she look like?"

He grinned at her. "The question every woman asks."

Alex stiffened a bit. "I didn't know it was a story you told so often."

"I don't, but women are so curious about how others look."

"Weren't you curious about Win?"

"No, I knew he was a wimp."

"Thanks a lot," she bristled.

He enjoyed her annoyance enough that his mood changed to one of comparative lightheartedness. "It's really quite easy for me to talk about Diana, you know, except for the part where she played me for such a sucker. All she hurt was my pride, really, and I probably had that coming.

"She had one of those dumb society girl nicknames I hated, Dee Dee, for her initials. I never called her that." He seemed to be thinking out loud. "She looked a lot like Robin Rhodes—same type, thin, blond, and expensive."

Alex felt her stomach muscles constrict. She looked

outside. Cassie was right. She'd been a fool. Turned down by Diana, he could now pick up the pieces of his bucolic dream with her clone, Robin Rhodes. Robin would be delighted to star in the rerun. Men always did that, she'd heard. If thin, expensive blondes were their type, they shopped till they found one who would take them on. Rod had come to the right place to get his wounded pride mended, she thought. Just my luck. Even if I starve myself, I'll never have that androgynous, slim-hipped-boy look that Robin has. Damn.

For Alex, the magic of the day was gone. She watched the miles tear by her low window, bleakly thinking she would have to redouble her vigilance to keep from falling in love with Rod. She would get two things out of this season with him—money from their vastly increased business, and knowledge. She could learn a lot from Rod, enough probably so that after he was gone she could keep some of the business for the farm. She'd have to work at learning as much as possible from him, all the while keeping up her guard against his charm—not an easy task.

Released from their harrowing conversation, Alex gazed out the window and let her mind wander, rewriting history. Instead of giving Rod an angry refusal of his unspoken request for protection from the local predatory females, in her daydream she gave him the kind of amused, cool, but positive response he admired. From that new beginning she imagined an ironic courtship, with herself fully in control, cresting to a climax of love when Rod, worn down by her enchanting coolness, realized she was his heart's desire.

Although mentally committed to her reverie, Alex kept track of the route and roused herself in time to warn Rod well before their exit. She took the written directions from her purse and sat up alertly to guide him to the stable. They were expected, so after introductions and a few preliminaries, they watched the horses in question go through their paces. Rod dismissed one out of hand but asked to ride the other. He put the young Thoroughbred mare through a few easy jumps, then asked that the bar be raised to four feet.

"I don't think she'll do that," the first rider warned as he put the bar in place.

She did. Rod let the horse sidle to Alex. "Try her," he said, getting off. Alex shook her head, thinking for once of her wardrobe rather than business.

As they returned to the car, Alex grinned at Rod. "Who was that masked man?"

"Do you have a firm price? It may go up."

"It won't. I've dealt here before. They know me." Alex was proud of her ability to bargain, of winning respect despite being both young and female.

Inside the car Rod asked, "Why didn't you try her? You have on pants."

She wrinkled her nose. "Because our next stop is an inn I know, where we're going to have lunch."

"You mean *you're* going to have lunch. They won't let me in."

"They'd let you in here *on* a horse. I went to boarding school with the owners' daughter."

"I keep forgetting your present poverty is new to you."

"You wouldn't call me poor if you read some of the offers I get for the farm from developers. Do you have any idea what seventeen acres of developable land is worth in Concord?"

"Then why didn't it go for that when you bought it?"

"As agricultural land it's priced differently, and Emma

Brody was fanatical about keeping it as a farm. Thank God." She pointed out a left turn for them to take. "I can sell anytime I want though."

"But you won't."

"No. Nevertheless, some nights I go to sleep thinking about all that money. It makes a nice change from worrying about all those bills."

Rod clucked disapprovingly. "What a waste. A beautiful woman like you should have something to keep her mind off such matters in bed."

Alex was able to minimize her flare of embarrassment by guiding Rod with unnecessary explicitness to a parking place in the inn's side yard. On the other hand, he made no attempt to hide his obvious amusement at her reaction. She knew that as long as she continued to blush she was going to be bombarded by similarly suggestive remarks. If only there were a way to short out the nervous connection that gave away her reactions.

Inside, Nell's parents escorted them like royalty to a sunny porch table looking over a small herb garden rimmed with climbing red roses. Before they could look at the menu, they received a complimentary bottle of Chablis and servings of hot spinach quiche. Unable to offend such kindness, Alex threw away her stricture about drinking wine in Rod's presence.

"Shall we drink to Mayfair Lady?" she asked, referring to the mare they had just seen.

He made a face. "That name has to go." He touched her glass with his. "I'd rather drink to ladies who blush."

She made a face back. "I'd rather not blush, you know," she said, doing so. "If only you wouldn't say such things."

"Everything I say is true. It's just rare to find such responsiveness today."

He was making it worse. She took a swallow of the warming wine—again on an empty stomach, she remembered too late. She put her glass down and took off her jacket, shrugging it onto the back of her chair. Another mistake. His eyes were frankly admiring.

"I've been waiting for that to come off," he said. "We'll have to have another toast. To sweaters with holes."

"Rod, be civilized," she squeaked, dismayed.

He laughed shortly. "I am, but just barely."

Nell's father came himself to take their order and, since neither of them had looked at the menu, Alex suggested he surprise them. After telling them about Nell's new baby, predictably producing pictures for their admiration, he went away and Alex steered the conversation to the neutral but mutually interesting topic of horses. They compared notes on amusing or inappropriate names for horses and were soon laughing wholeheartedly.

Their surprise was shepherd's pie, tender chunks of lamb delicately flavored with herbs in a flaky crust. "This sure beats life on the heartburn circuit," Rod said. "And in 'this' I include Miriam's meals as well. I'm going to have to start fasting or something pretty soon, or I won't fit into any of my clothes."

"Join the rest of us in the real world," Alex replied. "But just try even saying the word *diet* around Miriam."

"At least on you it settles in delightful places."

"You're doing it again," she said, trying to forestall another blush.

He sat back, regarding her with interest. "Why does it bother you so much to be admired?"

She looked down at the food on her plate, then up. He was still watching her. "I'm just not used to it, I guess."

"Then you've been a recluse too long. You went to

college. You must have run into some normal red-blooded males along the way."

"I went to a girls' school."

"So did most of the girls I've known. That didn't hold them back. Did you hide?"

"Basically I guess I did."

He smiled broadly. "Now I know why I was sent to Concord. Rod to the rescue."

She put up her hand. "Ho, right there."

"I'm not a horse, Alex," he laughed.

"If you were, I'd sell you," she flared.

"No, you wouldn't."

"We have a business relationship." Back to square one. Maybe if she said it often enough it would remain true.

"So? That doesn't mean we couldn't have fun."

"You'd have fun. I'd be miserable."

"No, you wouldn't. Guaranteed."

"You really are insufferable."

He smiled. "So I've been told."

"Love-'em-and-leave-'em Gilbert." She shook her head. "That's not for me. When you move on, I've still got to live in Concord. I need my reputation."

"Don't you know just having me there has already cooked that?"

"What?"

"We are living in the same house, Alex. Don't you think my fans have already wagged their tongues about that?"

She stared at him. "We're not even alone."

He laughed. "Robin thinks Miriam is deaf."

"That's not true."

"Of course it's not true, but do you think that matters to a jealous female?"

61

"Tell her."

"The truth will make you free? Dear Alex, you really are a babe in the woods."

"Stop patronizing me."

"I'm not patronizing you, at least not much. I'm telling you what's what. If you're keeping me at bay because of what others might say, you're wasting your energy—energy we could put to better use."

"Rod, stop it." She was getting tired of his relentlessness. "You're just saying all this because it suits your purpose."

"I don't deny that. But it doesn't keep it from being true." He finished off the wine. "Ask around. You'll see."

"I will."

"And then?"

"Then nothing. Even if it is true, it doesn't make it right. Or smart."

"And being right and smart is so important to you?"

"Yes, it is."

He nodded. "Okay. But I'm going to keep on asking, Alex, because I want you." He fiddled with his glass, watching her. "I think you want me too."

"You can't imagine otherwise, can you?"

"Oh, sure, I can. Even I strike out once in a while, especially with schoolteachers," he acknowledged. "But I'll keep trying."

To combat the look in his brown eyes and the effects of the wine, Alex asked for coffee. It didn't really help, and the rest of the trip to North Adams was a blur. They didn't find another good prospect, so that part of the jaunt was a waste of time, except that it gave Alex another opportunity to watch Rod evaluate a horse.

As she well knew, he did indeed have a knack for dealing with horses. She watched his hands moving over the animal, sure but gentle, checking for abnormalities, calming and reassuring as he patted a flank and rubbed a neck. He always got the best from a horse, sometimes, as with Mayfair Lady, exceeding what others believed possible.

Back in the car again, she continued to watch his hands as he drove, remembering the feeling of them on her bare shoulders at Henry's party. It was the wine, she reminded herself, trying to break the spell he had cast over her. They had already exhausted the topic of the horses they had seen, and Alex could think of no way to ask him the questions she wanted answered, so she dragged her eyes to the road ahead and tried to settle into another anesthetizing daydream.

"What do you think about when you look like that?" Rod asked, breaking into her consciousness.

Since she had just begun to replay their lunch conversation, she knew she would blush. "I guess I'm half asleep from the wine," she fudged.

"You were smiling."

"Was I?" She couldn't think of anything to say.

"Tell me. Do you ever wear your hair down?"

"Down? Well, yes, most of the time, really."

"Not just down, but loose and long. It's such pretty hair, but you always have it all zipped up in a braid or a twist of some kind."

"Usually I'm working and it gets in my way."

"And today?"

"I'm working now too," she reminded him, but then, because that sounded a bit like a rebuke, she added, "I look too young with it long. This way the men I meet will take me seriously. I try to make it look pretty . . ."

He responded quickly to the defensive note in her voice. "Oh, it's very pretty the way you wrap it like that. It's just that I'd like to see it loose sometime."

She didn't look at him. "Okay," she said softly.

"Sometime like when you go to the movies with me," he said.

She looked over at him quickly. He was giving her his amused but watchful smile, testing her reaction. Before she could decide what to say, he added, "Like tonight."

"What would Robin think of that?"

"Who cares? I made exactly the arrangement with her that I almost asked you about."

"You didn't dress it up any?"

"Why should I? She doesn't care. She's getting what she wants, and so am I."

"Which is what?"

"Why do you care?" he countered.

"I guess I don't," she lied, "except that if you have an understanding with her I wouldn't want to . . ." She petered off, looking away.

"Let me worry about that."

"Even so, it's not a good idea for us to go out together. I just don't want to get involved personally when we have to work together."

He sighed. "So you've said." His eyes went back to the road.

Had she refused? She stared out the window wanly, upbraiding herself for such colossal stupidity. Maybe it was the wine talking, at least inside, but she hadn't meant to turn him down. What she'd intended, she realized, was to state all her objections so he could override them, giving her a chance to say yes with a clear conscience. But he'd stopped too soon.

Cassie was right. She was a fool. Nothing in her experience had prepared her for dealing with a man like Rod Gilbert. She guessed, too, sneaking a glance at his stony profile, that nothing in his experience had prepared him for someone like her. He was accustomed to being the one pursued. While he was willing to take certain steps in pursuit of her, he was put off by her reluctance. The fact that it was, in part, pretended reluctance never got through to him.

The problem was one of expectations. But how could she capitulate if he wouldn't storm the barriers? And did she really want to?

The answer to that was an emphatic yes. But the real question was, should she? Would it be wise? He said he wanted her. Even without much experience she knew that was a long way from a declaration of love. If she accepted his terms, wouldn't that mean kissing good-bye to any chance at that remote goal, along with her self-respect?

Or wasn't that the way things worked today? First came sex; then, sometimes, love. But was that what she wanted? And how could she ever know when her mind was a muddle and all she could think about was his hands?

Rod turned off the highway onto a secondary road. "I need a cup of coffee. That wine is still with me," he explained.

"Good idea," she agreed, watching the road for a likely stop. When they'd found their spot, refreshed themselves, and were about to start again, Alex gathered her courage and asked, "Did I turn down that invitation for the movies?"

He looked surprised. "I thought so."

She nodded, her daring slipping fast.

"Am I to suppose you're now reopening the question?"

"Would you go one more round with me if I changed the answer?"

A smile hovered around his mouth, fighting with the irritation in his eyes. "Alex, this is the twentieth century, the *late* twentieth century. It's only a movie, for heaven's sake. Those kinds of games went out at least a hundred years ago."

She nodded again, not meeting his eyes. "I'm sorry."

"Don't look so beat up," he muttered. "I'm sorry, I just don't know what to make of you. You're all prickly with objections and arguments. How am I supposed to know what you want?"

She continued to look at her hands in her lap. He reached to turn her face his way with one finger on the side of her chin. When she met his gaze, he leaned his elbow on the top of the steering wheel. She could see his exasperation melt away, replaced by amusement.

"Alex, I'm not used to women like you. You'll have to come partway to meet me. That is, if you want to meet me."

"I want to. I'm afraid I'll regret it, but I want to."

"For just a movie?"

"It's not just the movie. It's the collapse of all that separation of business and social life."

"You have to decide." His hand hovered between them.

"I think I just did when I reopened the question."

"Okay then. Will you go to the movies with me tonight —with your hair long and loose?"

She nodded. "Yes."

"Will you wear a skirt and that sweater?" He touched

the neck, running his fingertip just under the sweater edge, so it grazed her skin lightly. She closed her eyes and nodded.

She heard him shift in the car seat, so it was no surprise that his lips brushed hers, but lack of surprise did nothing to minimize their impact. She opened her eyes just long enough to see him as he drew back to look at her, then he kissed her parted lips again. This time his hand on her shoulder pulled her around to face him and she was lost in warmth.

He broke off suddenly with a soft curse that startled her until she opened her eyes and saw the way he was leaning over the gear box to reach her. He gave her a look so charged it should have sent her flying from the car as he announced, "Tonight we take your car."

He backed out of the parking place then, leaving Alex to collect mind and body as best she could for the drive home. If she had wanted to pretend nothing much had changed between them, the first time he reached to touch her shoulder or knee would have dispelled that illusion.

By the time they were pulling into the farm driveway, Alex could barely control her rising alarm. She got out of the car and stretched to relieve her tension. When she turned back to the car, Rod was leaning on the roof, watching and grinning.

She dove back into the car for her purse and jacket, hissing at him, "Rod, stop it."

She started immediately for the house to change her clothes in order to help with the late feeding. He gave a low but carrying wolf whistle, and she had to force herself to continue going. Inside, she dashed up the stairs to her room, hoping for better composure before she faced all those prying eyes. Supper, unless he reformed—which she knew would never happen—would be murder. She wanted very much to regret letting him get his foot in the door as he did, but her heart wasn't it it.

However it turned out, it was out of her hands now. Thank goodness.

CHAPTER THREE

Alex endured supper as best she could. Knowing she was giving away the story by her embarrassment more than Rod was with his leers didn't prevent her from reacting anyway. He wasn't behaving differently; she was. And somehow the fact that she was to blame made it worse. Cassie and Ellen exchanged amused looks with impunity and after Rod left for the barn again. Alex tried also to escape to her office.

"Oh, no, you don't," Ellen said. She rolled her wheelchair to the doorway, laughing as Miriam took Rod's place at the table and began the interrogation.

"So what happened?" Miriam demanded.

Alex opened her mouth and Cassie put in, "And we don't mean about the horses."

"Well, we had a nice day."

They stared her down.

"Really, it was nothing much, except that I said I'd go to the movies with him. Really, that's all."

69

"Then why are you acting so embarrassed?" Cassie asked.

"He just upsets me the way he teases all the time. I don't know what to make of him. You all know that."

"Will you go out with him again?" Miriam asked.

"I don't know. Good grief, I haven't even gone out once yet. Maybe it'll bomb."

Ellen shook her head. "You'd better not blow this one, honey."

"Look, all of you, just back off a bit, will you? I know you mean well, but you make me feel so awful."

Ellen softened. "Hey, you know?" she asked the others. "She's right. We aren't helping very much."

"I'm not sure anyone can help me," Alex admitted. "I'm so scared I'm doing the wrong thing. I want to go out with Rod, but I know he's way out of my league. I just feel like I'm asking for trouble."

Cassie waved that aside impatiently. "What are you going to wear?"

"He told me what to wear."

They all stared at her.

"I'm supposed to wear my hair down. Loose."

They began to giggle, first Cassie, then the others, Alex with them. Miriam laughed so hard she rested her head on the table. Finally Alex tried to regain her control, wiping her eyes. "Please. You guys be somewhere else when we leave tonight, okay? I just about died this morning."

Cassie calmed next. "But you did so well. You looked fantastic."

Ellen asked, "When you take your hair out of that twist, is it curly?"

She shrugged. "Who knows? I'll have to go see."

"Go," urged Miriam. "We'll do the dishes and then scram."

They all nodded. Cassie said, "If you want a hand, give a holler in a half hour. If not, I'll go then."

"And we won't grill you like this all the time," Ellen promised.

"It's okay. You're all really sweet."

She didn't need anyone's help with her hair, opting for a half-up, half-down hairdo that pulled the front hair back along the sides of her head to braid into the back section and hang loose, as directed. She had a pretty camel-colored skirt to wear, so the only other decision involved her feet. She had nice dress boots she rarely got to wear, but somehow she knew Rod wouldn't care for that. She rejected the gold sandals as inappropriate, but then came back to them after looking at her brown pumps. At least the sandals weren't glittery, she decided, getting a head-to-toe view in her bedroom mirror.

Rod's knock on her door brought her up short. She went to the living room and opened it. He was carrying his blazer over his shoulder by one finger, dressed as he had been before in duplicate chinos and a tattersall shirt rolled back at the sleeves.

He stepped inside and looked her over, starting with her hair. "Very nice," he approved. She stepped back a bit. She found him disconcerting enough pinned behind the wheel of a car, but standing at close range he made her feel almost faint.

"I'd better get a sweater," she said, nodding at his jacket.

He caught her wrist. "No sweater. I'll keep you warm."

"Rod," she began as he tossed his blazer onto a chair and took her into his arms. Without the interference of a

71

gear box between them he pressed her tight against him from knee to shoulder, kissing her with breathtaking thoroughness. She put her hands on his chest, as if she would push him away, but that was far from her intention. When he lifted his face away, she didn't move for several long seconds. Finally she pushed back and he let her go.

"There was no one downstairs to announce me," he said, beginning to look around her room. "Your parents' things. They're beautiful. This is very nice."

"Thanks. Shall we go?"

He sighed. "I suppose so. I did promise you a movie, didn't I?"

The movie, about which she was not consulted, was a spy thriller that alternated fistfights with steamy and improbable love scenes. Rod devoured popcorn nonstop throughout, the rate of intake upping perceptibly during love scenes, only to slacken during the fights because he was too involved in the battles to remember to eat. He actually twitched in his seat as if he were taking and giving blows, much to Alex's amusement. Once or twice he patted her arm with a buttery hand, but otherwise she was left to her own devices. When the lights came on she expected him to be surprised to find her there, but he wasn't.

"That was great, wasn't it?" It wasn't an honest request for her opinion, so Alex said nothing.

Going up the aisle again, he touched her arm and she slipped away, which, given his condition, wasn't hard. "You're all butter to your elbows, Rod," she laughed.

He looked at his hands. "So I am. I'll wash up."

She raised a glistening arm and said, "So will I."

She found him again at the concession stand looking at the popcorn. "Don't you dare," she warned, taking his arm and leading him away.

"Don't you like popcorn?"

"Not as much as you do."

The midnight air was cool on her arms, so she welcomed his arm over her shoulder. In the car he tossed his blazer to her from the back seat. "You can wear that while I have to drive, but when we stop, it has to come off."

He stopped at the inn and reclaimed the jacket.

"Why are we stopping here?"

"So I can ply you with spirits, my lovely." He got out and came around to her door.

"Rod, for heaven's sake. I have to get up early tomorrow morning. So do you."

"That's right, so we need something to help us sleep." She didn't move. "Want me to carry you?"

She got out. There were only a few men in the cocktail lounge, but the bartender remembered Rod from his Christmas stay there, and probably from the many evenings he'd taken his dates there, Alex thought. She was disapproving as he ordered, again without asking for her preference, and tried not to drink much of her wine. He watched her, laughing to himself.

"It's not funny, Rod. You don't need that drink, and neither do I."

"You need yours, but you're right, I don't need mine."

"Why do I need it?"

"I really like your hair like that."

"You didn't answer my question."

"Because I've noticed how wine affects you, makes you a little more relaxed, a little more like your new hairdo."

"Rod, we've had a nice day, please don't spoil it."

"Drink."

"No. Please take me home."

He tossed back his Scotch and dug into his pocket for

money to slap onto the table. She walked stiffly to the car and got in without waiting for him to open her door. When he was about to turn on the ignition, he changed his mind and reached out to pull her over to him. His kiss affected her as much as before, but she didn't allow herself to respond overtly.

When he let her go she endured his close-range inspection without saying anything. Finally he sighed and retired behind the wheel. He shook his head over her.

"I have to hand it to you, Alex. You really are the ultimate tease. You look like spun gold. Beautiful, just beautiful. It doesn't matter if your hair is up or down, whether you're in a gown or old jeans; you make my mouth go dry with wanting you. But that's not what you want. We're so out of phase, you don't even know what I'm talking about."

Alex turned her head away and slid as far from him as she could get. He looked over the wheel at the darkened street, at the heavy heads of rhododendron blooming along the front of the inn, but still he didn't start the car.

"What is it about you? What is it about *me* that turns you off so?" He turned to look at her again. "When I kissed you earlier tonight I could swear you liked it, but now . . ." He trailed off.

She stirred slightly, trying to make herself reach out to him. She licked her dry lips. "I still feel the same way."

"Which is what? How?"

She laughed a little. "Scared."

"Of me?"

"Yes."

"Alex, you're twenty-six years old, and even if you've been living under a rock you ought to know something about men."

74

"I don't though. Every date I've ever had has ended like this, but this is the first time . . ."

"The first time what?"

"The first time I've cared. And I didn't think it would be this way tonight. It's just that you surprised me that way."

"Buying you a drink?" He was incredulous.

"Just that I was expecting us to go home."

"And what? Were you going to invite me upstairs?"

"No."

"That's what I thought. Alex, I've played peekaboo with that sweater all day. I'm not very patient anymore."

"I know."

"And?"

"I don't know what to do."

"Let me show you. Let me love you."

"That's the first time you've used that word."

"What word? Love?" He grasped the steering wheel as if it were a life preserver. "Damn it, Alex. You want me to say I love you when I don't even know you yet."

"You want me to jump into bed with you when I don't even know you yet," she countered.

He shook his head wearily, finally laughing. "You've got to admit it would speed up our acquaintance."

She smiled, happy to see him less angry. "Look, Rod, I'm sorry about freezing up tonight. I know I'm a trial to you and I can't really promise that being patient will win you anything. I wouldn't really blame you if you decided I'm not worth the trouble. But I'll be honest with you, probably a lot more honest than I ought to be. I'm attracted to you. Enormously. It would be very easy to give in to you. But then what do I do when you leave?"

"When I leave? Next year?"

"Or whenever. You see, I don't really expect you to stay the summer."

"When you say patient, you mean *patient.*" He stared at her in dismay. "Meanwhile, what are we supposed to do? Neck?"

"I don't know. Just spend time together doing things, getting to know each other."

"I already work with you every day and eat most of my meals with you. I know enough about you to know I want you. What more is there?"

"There's a lot," Alex said, turning on the seat to face him squarely. "For one thing, I hate movies like we just saw, and I don't always want white wine to drink. You see, I like to be consulted about things that have to do with me and my preferences."

He was surprised. "You always drink white wine."

"Not always. I did at Henry's, and today it was a gift. But tonight I should have been asked."

"Dear God. Is that why you were miffed?"

"It's not *why,* just part of the why. You have to admit you paid no attention to me and what I might have liked to do or have to eat or have to drink the whole evening. Then when I don't fall down dead from gratitude for the pleasure of being allowed to be in your company, you call me the ultimate tease. The whole thing just leaves a lot to be desired, Rod."

He looked at her, his expression warring between annoyance and wonder before his sense of humor took over and he began to laugh. "You really are something else, Alex. You know that?"

"I'm not just another pretty face."

He sat back against the door and looked at her. "You

76

sure aren't. Well, I suppose I had it coming. What are we supposed to do now? Go to ballets and poetry readings?"

"You couldn't dislike them more than I hate movies like we just saw."

"Then I owe you one evening doing something I hate. Okay?"

"That's a start. Thank you. Now I'd like you to drive us home."

"Okay, Alex, whatever you say." He started the car.

She laughed. "You don't have to be totally meek."

"We aren't home yet," he warned.

Alex had edged close to Rod, but she reversed her direction, saying, "Oh, oh." He put his arm over her shoulder and brought her back for the remainder of the drive.

Inside the front door Alex was torn between inviting him to the comfort of her living room and insisting that they stay on neutral but more uncomfortable territory downstairs. He folded his arms over his chest and watched the battle as it was played out on her features. She cocked her head to look up at him speculatively, her mouth in a small smile. "Would you like to come up for a drink?"

He leaned back against the front door. "Do you have any idea how provocative you look right now?"

She straightened instantly, folded her arms to match his, and snapped, "I guess not."

He touched her elbows, holding her lightly. "I didn't say that to be smart, you know. I was giving you some information." He turned her toward the stairs, giving a small push on her back. "I accept. Go on." He followed her inside her living room and took a seat on a plump couch. He still wore his blazer.

Alex hovered. "Do you want a drink?"

"Do you have ice?"

"I have a small refrigerator in the bedroom. Yes, I have ice."

"Okay. Scotch."

"Water? Soda?"

"Rocks." Rod watched her go into the bedroom, then looked at the living room. The furniture was grander than the room, but by not crowding the pieces and keeping them small in scale she had managed to avoid the look of a storage room filled with survivors of a better time.

She came back with two squat glasses and put Scotch into both from a lift-top cabinet.

"Now I'll know where to come when I'm thirsty," he said as she gave him the less-filled glass. "What do you have?"

"Scotch and club soda. But I don't always have the same thing, in case you're taking notes."

"I already have that piece of information filed away." He took a drink. "Why did you ask me up here?"

"To be comfortable."

"What happened to 'We both have to get up early tomorrow'?"

She made a face. "It's not that late. That was my panic talking." She put her drink onto a leather-topped coffee table, carefully using a coaster and providing one for him. "What did you mean by that remark downstairs?"

"About you looking sexy?"

"You said provocative."

"I didn't want to offend you."

"You said it was for my information."

"I have the feeling that you're pretty unconscious of the way you look and even the way you behave sometimes. From anyone else I'd figure she knew what she was doing, but the way you cry foul has me convinced that you don't mean to send out the signals you do."

"What do you mean by signals?"

"Take downstairs. That's a pretty classic line and it's usually an invitation for much more than a drink. Then you tipped your head and smiled up at me. The word that comes to mind is coy. Whether you meant it or not, the whole performance wasn't calculated to lower my thermostat."

Alex looked at him with rounded, solemn eyes. "I'm sorry. I didn't mean to."

"That's what I mean by signals. Generally it's all a guy has to go on. Over the years I've learned certain things a woman does mean certain things. The exception is with young girls, fourteen or fifteen years old. They sometimes try out something to see what will happen, then when it happens they're not prepared."

"You're saying I'm like a fourteen-year-old?" Alex was appalled.

"In some ways. That's why I've had trouble reading you. You're a mature woman. Obviously you manage your life very well in most of the ordinary ways. You're intelligent, fun to talk to, so I assumed you were all of a piece—a little shy, yes. But I didn't understand that you didn't mean half of what your body is saying."

"My body!" It was getting worse and worse.

"Does even the word scare you? You do have a body; everyone does."

"Rod, for heaven's sake." She took up her drink again.

"I'm trying to understand, you know." He sounded exasperated. "It's called body language."

"Rod, I'm not stupid."

79

"I know you're not. That's what makes this all so odd. You must know what a sexy body you have."

She made a dismissive move, putting her glass down with a thump.

"No, Alex, don't play games. You know. Or why would you wear a dress like that gold one? Or a sweater like this one, as a matter of fact, and without a bra?"

"Rod!" Her voice squeaked in embarrassment.

"I mean it. I'm not trying to embarrass you; I'm trying to figure you out."

Her face was flaming red, but some of that was caused by a rising tide of anger. "I am wearing a bra," she insisted.

That stopped him cold. "I don't believe it."

"Well, I'm not going to show you, if that's what you want."

He laughed. "You mean I've been trying all day to line up the holes just right for nothing?"

"Rod!"

"Well, what do you expect? What did you think I'd be doing when you chose that to wear this morning?"

"I just thought it was pretty and that you'd like it." Her tone was defensive.

"It is and I do. But you also knew it was sexy. Admit it."

"Well, what if I did? I have a right to be as attractive as I can be."

"And I'm going to react."

"Okay. You've made your point. From now on I'll go around wearing shapeless old sacks."

"Not my point at all." He put down his drink and reached a hand to her. "I'm not criticizing you. Just trying

80

to explain my lechery." He gathered her to his chest, kissing the side of her head above her ear.

"Anyway, it doesn't make any difference," she said. "I'm not your type anyway."

He pulled back and peered at her face. "What's that supposed to mean?"

"Thin, expensive, and blond," she reminded him belligerently. "Like Diana and Robin? You remember them?"

"And that's my type of woman?"

"Isn't it?"

He considered the question seriously. "No."

"I don't believe you. But even if I dieted like crazy I could never look like that."

"Why would you want to? Here you are with the Cadillac of bodies . . ."

"Yeah, well-padded . . ."

"Voluptuous is the word you're looking for."

"For a high school dropout you know a lot of words," she accused.

"It's the high-toned magazines I read. The ones with the pictures in the middle." He kissed her forehead, hands on her shoulders, and looked down at her, a fond expression on his face. "Alex, Alex, what am I supposed to do with you?"

"You could kiss me."

"I could do a lot of things." He closed his eyes for a few seconds, then, while she waited, opened them and said, "I could go downstairs a happy man if I could do one thing right now."

Alex's heart lurched. "What?"

"Just close your eyes and trust me."

She giggled. "Said the spider to the fly."

"Shut up."

She closed her eyes and held her breath. She felt his hands on either side of her head, sliding to the back. He was undoing the braid that held the front of her hair away from her face. He combed the hair down, his big fingers awkward but tender. She opened her eyes in time to see him bend to kiss her, his hands tangled in her long hair, holding her head still. She wanted to put her arms around him but the idea of moving seemed to violate a beautiful moment.

She opened her eyes to see Rod staring at her. "See? Necking's not so bad," she teased.

"Like overtures. They're nice, but I think you'll like the finale even more." He brushed her face with his bristly mouth, kissing the hollow of her cheek up to her eyes and down again to her waiting mouth. This time she put her arms around his shoulders as his arms wrapped around her. One hand moved on her back warmly, pressing her against his chest before it came to rest in the center of her back. He slipped one finger under the edge of her bra and stretched it. She pushed free.

"Just checking on your story," he laughed, getting to his feet and pulling her after him. He kissed her nose, patting her hair down around her face.

"Wear your hair down tomorrow, will you?"

She nodded and he let himself out.

Granting that request brought Alex a morning of egregious comment, as everyone from the oldest crew member to the driver of the grain truck making a delivery told her she'd never worn her hair down before. Between the remarks and the need to keep pushing the hair out of her eyes, she was ready to scream anyway by the time Rod caught her bending over, picking out a pony's hoof, and chose that moment to give her an affectionate pat that veered heartily toward a spank.

She gave him her dirtiest look. "Don't you ever do that again," she warned.

He grinned, leaning on a pitchfork beside her. "Why not?"

"I'm supposed to be in charge around here."

"No one saw me, boss lady."

"The walls and stalls have eyes and ears around here. There's no such thing as privacy in a barn like this and you know it," she lectured.

"If you hadn't screamed, it would have just sounded like me patting a horse."

"Thanks a lot."

"You look very pretty today." He looked pointedly at her hair.

"Well, enjoy it now because when I get to the house for lunch I'm tying my hair back. It's driving me crazy."

"It's driving me crazy too. I keep wanting to run my hands through it."

She looked at his hands and made a face.

He wiped them on his jeans, laughing. "I could wash them in the water barrel."

"Go earn your keep," she ordered, backing away to put the pony between them.

That afternoon she was checking the inventory of equine salves and ointments in the storeroom off the tack room, hair secured as promised in a low ponytail, when she heard a commotion in front of the barn. She went to the door, then on to the tack room window in time to see a car flash onto the road from the parking lot. It was a sound she feared, given the traffic of both horses and people around the barn, but she knew from past experience the offender would be long gone before she got to where she could get the car's number, so she returned to her list, hoping someone else would have taken down the license for the police.

The chore complete, she emerged from the storeroom in time to see Cassie's curly head bob into the tack room in obvious search. "Alex," she hailed, "did you see the fireworks?"

Alex frowned. "I heard a car, but I knew it would be gone before I could find out who it was."

Cassie's eyes glittered with excitement. "It was Robin Rhodes come to call on Rod."

Alex turned away to one of the tack boxes piled in the room. She looked warily at Cassie. "Why do I know I'm going to hear all about this from at least fourteen people today?"

"Because your name was mentioned several times, at top volume, I might add."

"Wonderful."

"I couldn't hear what Rod said. I don't think anyone but Robin could, but it must have been something. She took off like a rocket."

"Okay, Cassie. You've told me. Now are you happy?"

"Don't you even want to know what she called you?"

"Not particularly."

"Some of it wasn't too clear," Cassie admitted, "but I did hear 'brass-plated bitch' really well."

"Thanks. Now, will you leave or do I have to?"

"Okay, okay. Just remember, though, I had it first," Cassie grinned.

"Don't you always?"

"I try, kiddo." She wiggled her fingers good-bye and scurried off in search of another set of innocent ears.

Alex stayed on in the tack room, sitting on someone's storage box, trying to sort through her reactions. It was exactly the sort of thing she hated. Scenes and confrontations of all kinds bothered her, even almost frightened her. She knew it was too late to do anything about it. It was already part of the local mythology by now.

Obviously Rod hadn't quite known what he was getting into when he picked Robin to play games with. At some level he was trying to be a gentleman, so she couldn't really blame him for this. But it did rather taint their relationship, and she had no idea how to act now. Beyond ignoring it, of course, which would be her official stance.

The door pushed open again and this time it was Rod who vehemently kicked it shut behind him.

"Did you hear all that?"

"Just the highlights from Cassie."

"God, Alex, I'm sorry. I could have wrung her neck."

"You shouldn't be surprised. She's not one to go quietly."

"She said some pretty rotten things. I'm really sorry."

"I know you are. It's okay. People will consider the source, you know. Something better will come along and it will all be forgotten."

"Philosophical as hell, aren't you?"

"Aren't I?" She grinned at him. "I'm also mad as hell, but what can I do?"

"Who are you mad at?"

Alex considered. "Robin, a lot; you, a little."

"That's what I figured." He pulled her to her feet. "I'll let you take one free swing at me to get it out of your system." He folded his arms over his chest, bracing himself. "Go ahead."

Alex looked him over as if she were deciding where to strike. She smiled wickedly. "Close your eyes. Trust me."

He looked startled, then laughed, shrugging. When his eyes were closed she leaned onto her tiptoes and kissed him on the mouth softly. He was so rigid he almost fell forward in surprise. His arms went around her reflexively as his eyes flew open.

"A soft answer may sometimes turn away wrath, but usually it just makes the other person twice as mad."

"Not this time," Rod said, holding her against him. He rocked from side to side gently. "Alex, you know something? I like you."

Several flip retorts came to Alex's mind but she didn't give them voice, sensing that his admission was a milestone for him. "I like you too."

He let her go with a laugh then, stepping back. "Last night you had me necking like an excited eighth-grader, now I've slipped back to fourth grade."

"Third grade," she corrected him. "By fourth grade they say 'I love you.' Go get to work again."

"Are you going to hide in here?"

"Nope. I'm getting tack together for my next lesson."

"Okay. See you at supper."

Alex went to the house in answer to the dinner bell, knowing there would be enormous curiosity about her reaction to the incident with Robin. What surprised her more than anything was how little it bothered her, any of it. Somehow the fact that Rod had sought her out to apologize made all the difference. She felt comfortable with him for the first time and the rest of the crew didn't matter. All her priggish worry about what everyone would think fell away, leaving her with a clean sense of self-respect. At the earliest opportunity during the meal she alluded humorously to the incident, effectively sweeping it into the ashcan, to everyone's relief.

She followed Ellen into her room off the kitchen when clean-up was over and plunked herself onto the bed.

"Being in love agrees with you, Alex," Ellen said. "We were all worried about what this would do to you. But you've changed. Overnight."

"Well, if I have, it's not because of what you think."

Ellen's eyes widened innocently. "What would I think?"

Alex laughed nastily. "About the same thing Robin thought. But I really don't care."

"Good. As long as you're happy."

"I'm getting there, but I'm in no hurry."

"He's a nice guy, Alex." Ellen looked down at her hands, the right one on top of the twisted, useless left one. "Did he tell you he wants to put a plywood path over to the barn for me, so I can watch the shows and lessons?"

Alex sat up. "What a great idea. Now, why didn't I think of that?"

Ellen laughed a little. "You wouldn't mind it? All those boards around?"

Tears came to Alex's eyes. "Ellen, love. Mind? I just never thought . . . and I should have. Why am I so stupid?"

"You're not stupid. You're my best friend. If it weren't for you, I'd never see anything but the back room of my parents' house."

"Big deal. You dare be grateful and I'll bop you one." She looked at Ellen fiercely. "Maybe you could get a motorized chair. They have those."

"Then I could tool up the highway like Robin Rhodes."

"Please. Spare me," Alex laughed. "Look, I came to ask you if you'd teach me to play rummy too."

"How come? You never wanted to play before."

"I thought only two could play, and you guys seemed to be all set."

"But Rod plays, so you want to."

"It would be horning in, wouldn't it? I'm sorry. I wasn't thinking from your side."

"It's no big deal."

"No, forget it. I was just trying to think of things to do with him that were just . . . I don't know."

"Not sexually charged?" Ellen grinned knowingly.

Alex laughed. "Maybe there's no such thing with him."

"No, I don't think there is. You might as well give up and give in."

She looked sharply at Ellen. "You really mean that."

"Of course I do and it's the best advice you'll ever get."

"But what about when he goes?"

"Better to have loved and lost? Remember that? And who knows? You might not lose."

"He'll go back to the big-time."

"So? Are you cast in concrete? You could go too."

"Two problems. He'd have to want me to and . . ."

"The farm," Ellen finished for her. "That's really only one problem because the farm isn't a living, breathing person, however devoted to it you are. If the time ever comes, I'll kick your fanny all the way to New York after him."

"Then we definitely need to get you a motorized buggy, lady. And a *long* plywood path."

The plywood path didn't reach quite to New York, but it got Ellen into the heart of the barn action again. With the addition of a ramp or two here and there and the subtraction of an occasional threshold, the entire first floor, including the indoor ring, was made accessible to Ellen's wheelchair. Since there was little she didn't know about riding from her years of lessons and competition, she was soon able to teach classes and supervise a myriad of procedures others found onerous. It was like gaining two extra experienced workers, just at the crucial time, as the show season began to move into high gear.

With Rod and his new horses to show, the entire season took on added luster. For many of the riders it marked the first time they would compete in rated, sanctioned shows. Understandably, they were nervous and excited. Preparations began early in the week as the horses were groomed, brushed, and combed, their manes braided with colored yarn, their tails brushed plumy. Riders and their grooms began arriving on Saturday morning before dawn for some day trips in order to wrap protective bandages around their horses' fragile legs before they were loaded into the vans.

Later the riders themselves would give their own appearance attention, not as much as they gave their pampered mounts, but enough to transform apparently grubby stablehands into equestrians. Alex loved to see her pupils turned out in buff breeches, gleaming boots, and handsome black jackets, topped by the protective hard hat, a black velvet dome that made the lowliest rider look like royalty.

For Alex, each horse show was a combination carnival, circus, and college final exam. She was especially aware of the test element at their first big show, knowing their little band of competitors would be judged severely because of Rod's reputation. Fair or not, they would all be expected to perform well. Then, too, Rod would be judging them by another set of standards. Were they worth his time? Even if they won every class, even if they swept the show, they might still fail to meet Rod's expectations. And that concerned Alex the most.

The day was warm and sunny but not hot, a blessing in view of the fact that only a few people could find shade, and that only when they weren't busy preparing for a class or helping another prepare. Although Alex had her own responsibilities, she was able to observe Rod putting his riders through their paces, exercising the horses, checking out the courses each would ride. Wherever course plans were posted to a tent pole or tree, a cluster of riders stood memorizing the order and arrangement of fences before they walked the course, pacing off distances and plotting strategies for getting their particular horses over the hurdles without incident.

Incident, as Rod reminded his jumpers, meant either having the horse refuse to jump the fence, or knocking down a bar, not ticking or hitting a bar or part of the structure.

"I don't care what you hit or how often," he directed, "as long as you leave it standing." In addition to his general advice, he had specific instructions for each rider and a joke to help ease each one's tensions. One by one the results began to pile up in colorful ribbons of blue, red, and yellow.

The highlight of the day, however, came when Rod took one of the relatively green but promising horses, an Arabian gelding, through the most difficult course of the day in a silky exhibition of pacing and horsemanship that brought a spontaneous round of applause from the knowledgeable audience. Alex was breathless with admiration but aware enough that her emotion was shared by every female there, so that she immediately turned away and returned to one of the vans rather than stand in line to gush over Rod.

When Cassie came upon her carrying water to one of the horses ten minutes later, she was irate. "Don't tell me you've been back here the whole time and missed Rod's ride."

"I saw it, Cassie."

"Aren't you the cool one though?"

"What do you expect me to do? Fall all over him?"

"Why not? He's knee deep in fans. Don't you think he'll wonder whether you care?"

"I'll tell him, Cassie. Just not now." She continued to work until Cassie left, then she went into the van to check on the hay. She rattled down the metal ramp from the van just as Rod handed the reins to one of the youngsters and gave the horse a dismissive pat on the rump.

He turned to her, enveloping her sweatiness in a bear hug. "Women and horses," he said, laughing into her neck, "you sweet-talk 'em at one end and smack 'em at the other."

"You sound pleased," she said, trying to dance away from his reach in case he decided to demonstrate the second part of that statement. "You're going to get hooked on adulation."

"I already am," he beamed. "What a super job the kids did."

"Your performance wasn't half bad either. Do you suppose you could teach me to ride like that?"

"Maybe." He measured her with his eyes seriously. "But you have to learn how to sit on the horse first."

"Rod!" She was aghast. She knew she was a long way from being a great rider, but to be told she didn't sit right

91

was beyond belief. She searched his eyes for the giveaway twinkle that meant he was teasing. "You mean that, don't you?"

"I always mean what I say, especially to you."

"What's wrong with my seat?" The term was correct, but as soon as the words were out she knew she had asked for trouble.

"Your seat is adorable," he said, smiling in recognition of the way she'd walked into that comment, "but you perch up there like a schoolteacher, all prim and mannerly, instead of getting down into it and becoming part of the horse." He grinned finally. "Once you get rid of a few more inhibitions you'll be a better rider."

"One-track mind," she sniffed.

"Hey, when it's the right track, why change?" He looked around the van. "What does a man have to do around here to get a drink?"

"Horses get water; a man has to leg it over to the concession stand and buy a Coke."

"Boy, you're cute all hot and sweaty, you know that? Want to go skinny-dipping in the pasture pond with me when we get home?"

"Yuck. You haven't looked too deeply into the pond, I can tell."

"No imagination, that's your problem."

"Too much imagination is my problem, but if you want to swim tonight, we can probably go to Walden Pond. But first I'll find you a Coke."

He sat down on the ramp, stretching his long legs before him. "Now I remember why I like it here."

"Just don't change your mind before I get back."

Even though she hurried, he was gone when she got back. A squashed Coke can sitting on the ramp told her he'd appropriated a soda from one of the kids and had gone on his way. Nevertheless, the happy glow left over from their conversation remained to warm her heart. He was pleased. They had passed through another barrier and she could let go of another chunk of her resistance to him. Like the last clump of snow on a spring day, the last of her defenses were rapidly melting.

And to think, he would suggest giving in to him would make her a better rider! For sheer gall, it was unsurpassed, she decided with a smile.

CHAPTER FOUR

By the time Alex drove into the yard that evening with her load of young riders, Rod and the older competitors were having a party. Ellen, who had been overseer for the day in their absence, was parked at the bottom of the main ramp to the barn, listening avidly to every detail of their triumph. She hailed Alex, inviting her to join them.

"Did you have a hard day?" Alex inquired, perching on the fence next to the wheelchair.

"Dull as dishwater, thank heavens. It was a day off."

"Good. We've been working you too hard." It was true. Since taking on so much responsibility, Ellen occasionally showed strain on her thin face. She no longer stayed up playing cards and watching TV with Miriam after dinner, but now was fast asleep by nine o'clock every night.

Rod handed Alex a can of beer, checking Ellen's for the need for a refill. Rod was back in jeans already, as were about half the others; those who were not, like Alex, were still in knee-high boots and riding breeches. Jackets were hung away long ago, and everywhere around her the once pristine ratcatchers, collarless riding shirts, were now badly wrinkled and grubby.

Alex loved this time almost more than any other at the barn, especially if the show had gone well. Even the few horses still being walked up and down were relaxed.

Ellen grinned up at where Alex sat. "I hear it was a triumph."

"Kinda. Yeah, it was great. You heard about Rod's ride, I'm sure."

"At least twenty times, but I'm good for another twenty more hearings probably."

Alex noted the shine in Ellen's dark eyes and laughed. "It's a good thing we don't have your motor scooter yet, or you'd be up for drunken driving tonight."

"You're right. But here's to it." She raised her beer can in her good hand, slopping some beer onto the ground.

Rod took it from her grasp and drank from it before handing it back to her with a kiss on the cheek. "Ellen, old girl, we can't take you anywhere," he scolded her.

She was not offended. "You know, Rod," she said with a calculating look at Alex, "we used to have a tradition around here of dunking the boss in the water barrel after a winning show."

Alex straightened in a hurry. "Ellen!" she squealed. "You traitor!"

Before she could jump from the fence, Rod grabbed her, lifting her easily by the waist. He put her over his shoulder in a fireman's carry, one hand on her hip, the other holding the back of her knees. She pummeled his back and tried to kick, getting in a couple of cracks at his legs.

"Head first or feet first?" Rod asked, turning toward the barn.

"Who cares?" someone yelled.

She kicked Rod again, so he reached up and smacked with his opened hand at the seat of her tight breeches.

"Take off her boots," one of the girls called, mindful of their value.

"Good idea," Rod agreed. He sat on the ramp and levered her into his lap so she was sitting on him as if he were a chair, still holding her squirming body easily in his steely arms. She tried to kick the hands that grabbed her boots, but there were too many of them and with Rod bracing her against their force the high boots popped off.

If it hadn't been happening to her, Alex would never have believed Rod could get up from the ground and lift her at the same time, but he did it and carried her by the waist to the water barrel inside the barn door. A valve kept the water level in the barrel constant at close to the top, so buckets of water for the horses could be filled easily from one source. He lifted her over it and timed her feet-first dunk so that her feet were together when he lowered her.

The cold water splashed up to her chest, and the one consolation Alex had was that he got nearly as wet as she did from the barrel's runover and from her splashing. He did not push her head under but let go of her as soon as she was standing, dancing back from the cascading water around him. She scooped handfuls of water at him until he got beyond her range.

The metal barrel came to above her waist, making it awkward for her to climb out. She propped her hands on opposite edges, trying to extricate herself. Rod watched and came closer.

"Want some help?" he teased.

She splashed him again, but he came closer, laughing.

When he lifted her out, she made sure he got wetter, but she didn't try to keep him away.

"I'll get you for this, Rod," she threatened, laughing. "If I have to wait all summer, I'll get even." She began to shiver as the air hit her drenched body. She wrapped her arms around herself and ran down the ramp. "And you, Ellen!" she yelled, grabbing up her boots. "Your days are numbered!" She ran to the house. She padded, wet, up the stairs straight to her bedroom, where she dropped the boots. She caught a glimpse of herself in the full-length mirror behind the door.

"Dear me," she said, holding out her arms. "I might as well be naked." The soaked sleeveless cotton shirt clung to every inch of her torso, outlining even the edges of her bra. The stretch breeches, revealing enough dry, did the same for the rest of her body. At least her hair was still dry, except for a splash or two.

She scampered to the bathroom, peeling off the soggy clothes as she ran the water for a shower, and put them into the sink in deference to the rest of the bathroom. The change from icy water to warm made her comfortable enough to begin plotting how she would get back at Rod. Because she couldn't simply muscle him as he did her, she would have to outsmart him—and then make a quick getaway. That would be the hardest part, she knew, unless her revenge rendered him unconscious. She giggled, planning one bizarre scheme after the other.

When she was dry she pulled on her short nightgown and went to the bureau for her hairbrush, letting her hair down as she went. When her hair was smooth she turned away, then stopped cold. She crept to the closed door of the living room, listening for the sound that had alerted her. Someone was in there. She was about to open the door

97

when she recalled her attire and backed away to reach her bathrobe. Then she opened the door.

Rod was sitting on the arm of the overstuffed couch, his brown arms crossed over his T-shirt, watching the door. He got to his feet as she steamed toward him. "What do you mean coming up here like this?" she squeaked, dismay ruining any chance she might have had at dignity or authority.

He put his hand over her mouth, laughing. "Shh. No one knows I'm up here, so if you're quiet no one will ever know."

She opened her mouth to bite his hand but he snatched it away. "You're drunk."

"Not at all." He sat back down. "I wanted to be sure you were okay."

She eyed him skeptically. "Sure you did."

"I asked you to go swimming, remember?" He reached behind him on the couch and brought up two cans of beer. "You never got all of your victory drink." He opened one and handed it to her. She took it and backed off.

"What happened to the party?"

"That was it. When you left, everyone split. I took Ellen home and turned her over to Miriam, got out of my wet things, and came to see you. You're not going to bed now, are you?"

She took a drink. "Not any more, obviously."

"Don't let me stop you." He looked at her robe pointedly. "Why don't you go put on something less disturbing to me."

"Because you're not staying."

"Sure I am."

"Rod, there are more people around here tonight than usual, and this is not where you should be."

98

"My room looks occupied. I left the shades pulled and the TV on. Anyway, why shouldn't I be up here with you? Come on and sit down. Talk to me. I'm all wound up. I couldn't go to sleep now if my life depended on it. If you don't want me to stay here, I'll go off and find company somewhere else."

"That sounds like a threat. Are you trying emotional blackmail now?"

"Do you think it would work?" He smiled, but Alex didn't like the edginess of the smile.

She smiled back, relenting. "Hold this. I'll be right back."

She went back to her bedroom and looked for some clothes to pull on quickly. She didn't like the way he had come up to her room, but perhaps, looked at from his point of view, there wasn't anything wrong with it. She sensed a kind of unease in his manner that disturbed her. She knew the way some people were affected by shows, but she couldn't imagine this one getting to Rod that way—certainly not after the Garden shows he'd been through. Distractedly she pulled on panties and cotton shorts, settling for a cool halter top she could wear without a bra. Only when she went out to the living room again did she realize her mistake.

He was standing to look out the back window and when he saw her his intake of breath was audible across the room.

"Oh, dear," she said quietly. "I wasn't thinking." She turned to go back again, but he came to her quickly, stopping her with his hand on her waist. The tips of his fingers, cold from holding the can of beer, touched her bare skin above the shorts. "I like the way you don't think," he said.

His voice sounded strange and his eyes were dark with pain. "Rod, what's wrong?" she asked, putting her hand on his cheek. "You look so unhappy."

He laughed tightly. "Do I?" He searched her face. "You really don't understand what you do to me, do you?"

She took her hand away quickly. "Oh, that."

He ran the other hand up her arm to rest on her bare shoulder. "Yes, Alex, that."

She knew she should move in some way to defuse the situation, but his hands, so light on her skin, seemed to render her will useless. She swayed, drawn to his mouth, to his dark eyes. "Rod, oh, Rod." She stretched up to him, offering her mouth to be kissed, but he didn't move.

Finally she could bear the distance between them no longer and she put her arms around his shoulders to pull him down to her mouth. She kissed him as he had so often kissed her, urgently, demanding a response. She could sense that his response was there, deep and strong, but he refused to give in to her.

"A taste of my own medicine?" she asked, backing down.

"Something like that."

"Harsh medicine."

"Is it? Isn't it what you want?"

"No."

"No? Then what do you want?"

"I don't know."

"You don't know, or you won't say?" he challenged her. "I think you want exactly what I want, you just don't want to take responsibility for it. You want me to pick you up and carry you to bed. You want me to overpower your flimsy excuses just the way I did earlier tonight, only instead of soaking you in water, you want me to make love to you, holding you down if necessary."

She couldn't look at him. She felt his eyes raking her face.

"It would be so easy, a fantasy come true." He took his hands away and stepped back, breaking the contact that was supporting her. She looked up in alarm.

"Rod, please."

"Please what?"

"Please don't be mad. Please don't go." Her eyes entreated him.

"That's not good enough. You're still playing games, Alex. I want a woman, not a little girl in a woman's body, no matter how great the body."

"You expect me to ask you? Just like that?" Alex could hardly ask even that. She wanted to hide her face against his chest, away from his searching eyes.

"Why not? You know I'm not going to turn you down." He lifted her face so she had to meet his eyes.

"Couldn't you just hold me?" She was afraid she was going to cry, something he'd never understand.

"I could hold you, I want to; but I can't *just* hold you."

She pushed past his hand and pressed against him with her arms around his back. "Then hold me, please," she said into his T-shirt. His arms folded around her without conviction, but were comfortingly there. Her hands followed the ridge of muscles across his back to his ribs, content to rest on him, feeling his lean warmth. She stood on tiptoes to reach his mouth, tracing the edge of his moustache with her lips, edging her hands over his chest to his neck. She kissed him as she had before, urging him to respond, to meet her halfway. His arms tightened and she settled her face into his neck.

"Ever hear of spontaneous combustion?" he asked.

"Wet hay causes it," she murmured.

He kissed her ear through her streaming hair. "So does a wet blouse."

"Can't blame me for that." She hung from him, her bare legs pressing against his.

He laughed. "Most fun I've had here."

"I'll get even."

"Not tonight, please."

She laughed, dropping down to look at his face. "That's revenge I hadn't thought of."

He pulled her hard against him, hands spread on her bare lower back, fingers reaching under the waistband of her shorts. She leaned up to kiss him, but he picked her up by the waist again, carrying her backward into her room as he had earlier to the water barrel. She didn't kick but rested her hands on the bunched muscles of his arms and shoulders. He pushed the door closed by leaning on it briefly before putting her onto the big four poster that had always been hers. He sat down beside her.

"You didn't scream."

"I'm screaming inside," she admitted. "But maybe I'm more afraid of Miriam than I am of you."

"I'm flattered."

"You should be." She ran her hands up his arms under the sleeves of his T-shirt. "You're stronger than she is, but she yells at me."

"Maybe I should try that."

"Uh-uh. I cry when I'm yelled at." She looked at his arms, at the brown hair curling over his forearms. "Do you have hair on your chest?" The question popped out before she could check it.

He laughed, nodding. "How about you?"

"Rod," she protested, giggling.

"Just wondering. How about I show you, then you show me?"

Embarrassed, Alex leaned forward to hide her face in his neck. He kissed her neck, pushing her hair back from her face, then kissing her eyes and the pulse of her temple. His hand went to the back of her neck, following the loop of cloth across her shoulders. The other hand searched across her back for a clasp.

He held her off to look at her. "Is this an IQ test or something?"

She laughed. "I'm not telling."

He ran one finger down the inside edge of the halter to the hollow between her breasts where the two sides fastened. She didn't breathe as he reached with both hands to undo the single clasp. He tugged, then pushed, then folded his arms across his chest, glaring at her. "You'd better help me, if you ever want to be able to wear that again."

She took his hands and tried to demonstrate the twisting motion needed, but there were too many hands. So she did it herself finally, then tried to lean forward against him. He held her firmly by one shoulder while he folded back first one piece of fabric, then the other, to reveal her full round breasts. Again she heard his sharp intake of breath that affected her more than any words he could say. She closed her eyes, turning her head to the side, as he simply looked at her. When he touched her at last, it was as if his eyes had become tactile, tracing the globular shape of her breasts in narrowing spirals, finally flicking with tantalizing lightness over their tight centers. All sensation focused on his hands and their exploration until he eased her back onto the bed, pulling the halter free from her

103

arms. Blindly, she reached out to him, seeking his closeness.

He sat on the edge of the bed, quickly ridding himself of his shoes and clothes. She waited, eyes closed, for him to hold her. When her arms went around him this time, she felt the bare hard muscles of his back. He propped himself on one elbow to take possession of her mouth, his lips and tongue demanding that she answer his need. When she touched the inside of his mouth with the tip of her tongue, his entire body tightened and he lowered his head to one breast, taking the nipple into his hot mouth. She moved as he had, a small moan of pleasure telling them both what she was feeling.

Without taking his mouth from her breast he unbuttoned and unzipped her shorts, pushing them down over her hips. He half sat up as she kicked off the shorts, looking at the length of her body in a lacy pair of bikinis he regarded with amusement. "Who would have thought my little schoolteacher would have such sexy underwear?"

"I like lace." Alex tried to pull him down to her, tried to embrace him again.

He kissed her but lifted himself away to look at her once more. "I want to see you. You're so lovely. I tried to imagine your breasts, their shape and color." She turned her head away, embarrassed, glad the only light came from the open bathroom door. "Don't turn away, Alex. I want you to know you're lovely. What I didn't think about was how delicate you are. Your waist is so small. I noticed that tonight, picking you up."

"I'll have bruises from your hands tomorrow," she laughed, opening her eyes enough to see him.

"Really?" His concern was genuine.

104

"Maybe not," she backtracked. "Anyway, I kicked you a lot."

"So you did." He kissed her nose. "Compared to the critters that kick me every day, it felt like nothing."

She put her face against his chest and then put her hands flat over the dark wings of hair across his chest before she rubbed back and forth, enjoying the texture of his hair under her hands. "You do have hair," she confirmed.

He touched her the same way. "And you don't."

She laughed, a little light-headed. She had tried to imagine lying like this with Rod, expecting to feel as excited as she was, but never picturing herself laughing companionably with him as if this were something familiar and easy as well as exciting. But then suddenly his hand dropped to her panties, escalating her temperature by several degrees. "Except here," he said.

He laughed as she moved under his hand. "I knew you were passionate," he exulted, his mouth warm and moist on her ear.

He rested on his side, facing her with one arm supporting her upper back so that the sweeping curve of her neck invited the exploration of his lips, from the smooth skin of her throat to the delicate half-circle of her collarbone. She closed her eyes, not even daring to breathe as he slowly savored and tasted the vulnerable column with his softly bristled mouth. When his tongue probed the hollow at the base of her throat and lingered there, she tried to press against him and infect him with her growing sense of urgency. It was warming and wonderful the way he seemed to be worshiping her with his lips and tongue, but she'd already had a sample of the pull of his mouth on her breast and she was hungry for that, not this tantalizing almost-ness that made her feel deprived and restless. His big hand cupped her shoulder, holding her from behind, preventing her from insinuating herself closer. When she could do nothing else she snagged his top leg with her foot and as much of her leg as she could make reach him.

He raised his head and looked at her leg. Without releasing her shoulder, he lifted her knee away and held it against the bed. His hand burned against her skin and her eyes fluttered open. "Rod," she said weakly, moving her head from side to side in confusion.

"No, Alex. I'm not going to rush my fences. I've thought of nothing but this for too long." His eyes were black, the brown irises only thin circles around the devouring centers. His hand moved from her knee, the callused palm excitingly abrasive against the smooth skin of her inner thigh. "But I will take these away," he said of her bikinis, "because I want to see every inch of you."

She felt impaled by his eyes. She wanted to close her weighted eyelids and escape into the internal realm of sensation, where she could treasure and explore her body's response to the feeling of Rod's hands against her tremulousness. But as long as he looked into her flushed face, she was held, skewered by his piercing gaze. He seemed to see into her mind, to see more than the aroused surface of her body, and until he broke the contact she could only wait.

But then when he finally released her eyes to look down at the vulnerability of her revealed body, she no longer wanted to retreat or to withdraw into herself. Something of his desire to know her had been communicated. She wanted to see him, wanted to watch his face as he discovered the lushness of her femininity.

Her eyes were drawn from his face to the breadth of his

shoulders and the broad muscles of his chest, sculpted by years of hard physical labor. The tapered ruff of dark hair that graced his chest inevitably led her curiosity down over his lean stomach to confront the unabashed evidence of his arousal.

When she might have drawn back he gathered her quickly to his chest and covered her mouth with his. His tongue searched behind her teeth, not letting her retreat into timidity. "You're a woman, Alex, a glorious, golden woman. You make me glad I'm a man."

His words sent her senses eddying into a vortex of pure sensation where she was consumed by responsiveness to his every groaned command. "Trust me, Alex. I won't hurt you."

Only a small part of her mind needed the words of reassurance. Her body was lost to her control, driven by ever-escalating rhythms she responded to with mindless ecstasy. Each touch of his mouth, each nip of his torment-ing teeth, sent her up spiraling flights of stairs, each set steeper and more breathtaking than the last. At each pla-teau he gave her less and less time to regain her bearings, until finally she was lost, totally dependent on his strength and sureness.

She cried out in shocked reaction to the piercing sweet-ness released within her veins at the moment his decisive thrust of possession joined them into one throbbing being. His arms were all that held her secure as the world rocked around her. She clung to his shoulders, her mouth open in supplication under his, frozen, utterly suspended in time and space, until slowly he began to move in sweet persuasion, wooing her from within her own body, melt-ing her resistance.

Then she was swept away by delight. She heard him cry

her name hoarsely, heard her own answer torn from her throat in amazement, but nothing else was real to her until the last shudders died away within her and she found herself clinging to Rod like the lone survivor of a cataclysm.

As she slowly returned to consciousness, Alex became acutely aware that her face was pressed against Rod's damp chest, that her legs were tangled with his, that his hand rested intimately on her bare hip. A nervous giggle bubbled within her. "I hope Miriam really is deaf."

Rod's hand patted Alex in an automatic gesture of distracted comfort. "Did I hurt you?"

Alex didn't recognize her brittle laugh. "Do you hear me complaining?"

He eyed her suspiciously as she tried to extricate herself from his side, but he didn't keep her from moving away. "Maybe they caution men away from virgins because they're exhausting."

"All that pent-up emotion," she said as she resettled edgily next to him. Even in repose the obvious power of Rod's body made her wary. Part of her—most of her, in fact—wanted to nestle back against him, but instead she preserved a careful strip of separation between them that he instantly violated by rolling slightly toward her and looping a long arm over her waist.

"Now when you ride you'll know how to grip the horse with your legs," he teased.

"Rod!"

"That really gets you, doesn't it?"

"Well, of course it does. I teach people to ride, too, you know. I take pride in riding well."

"I've found something you do better."

"You're just saying that so you can come back and visit again."

He hooted with laughter. "Visit! I'm not going."

"Of course you are and pretty soon too."

"I like this bed better. Mine's too small and empty.

"Too bad. You're not moving in."

He gave her a quick kiss. "We'll see."

"Rod, I mean it." Alex sat up, looking at him seriously.

He reached out for her playfully. "How can I argue with you when you're all dressed up like this?"

She rose and walked away for her bathrobe. When she turned back he was pulling on his pants.

Alex felt confused. Nothing had been solved. They had made love—beautifully, if her senses and his words were to be believed—and yet they were now miles apart on yet another issue. Didn't all that passion and unity translate into anything else that mattered? Would he always escalate his demands so that as one was met another grew in its place?

Rod stood up, T-shirt in hand. He touched her shoulder. "You don't look very happy."

Unable to express herself, she simply stood.

He drew her to his chest. "Regrets?"

She sniffed, trying not to cry. He patted her hair awkwardly, then sat down, drawing her to sit on one knee. She put her head on his shoulder, disconsolate.

"Can you tell me what's wrong?"

She shook her head, sure she'd never be able to put her sadness into words.

"I didn't hurt you; you said that," he stated. "Maybe you're just sorry it's over." He peered at her face. "Are you?"

She nodded. "But that's not it." She lifted her head. "It didn't solve anything."

"Solve anything? I don't understand."

"I don't know. Two seconds later we were still disagreeing."

"Well, that's going to happen. I'm still going to be me; you're still going to be you."

"I know, but I thought we'd be different, closer."

"You don't feel closer?"

"I feel lonely." Alex had no idea where the words came from, but as she said them she knew they were true and the realization engulfed her with sadness greater than anything she'd felt since her parents died. In spite of everything she had felt with Rod, she was alone, just herself, isolated within her own skin, able to touch another only for a few fragile moments. Unstoppable tears flowed down her cheeks completely without her permission.

"Oh, Alex. I guess that's the way it is sometimes. I'm sorry."

"Do you feel lonely?" She was amazed to be able to talk while crying such torrents of tears.

Rod reached past her to grab tissues from her bedside table. "Not now, no. But I've felt something like that. It even has a name, I think, but I don't remember it." He mopped up her face, wearing a frown that might have been concern or just concentration. "I'm too selfish right now to feel anything but great. Sorry." His smile was a little self-effacing quirk.

When she was drier he lifted her to the bed, gently urging her to lie back beside him. "It helps just to stay close. You were so busy booting me out, you brought it on yourself."

She popped up. "There you go again. You just never let

110

up." She started to cry again, this time more her normal noisy self.

"Okay, okay," he soothed her. "I'll go whenever you say. Take it easy." He pillowed her head on his shoulder, his arms around her cotton robe. As before, his arms gave such comfort that she began to relax. She could feel the steady beat of his heart under the hand resting flat on his chest. His leg, even through the pants, was hard as a tree between her bare legs. She moved against him, burrowing closer to his comfort, her hand drifting down over his chest to the depression below his ribs.

He laughed softly. "You're really a very forward little girl, do you know that?"

She lifted her head to see his face. "I thought you didn't want a little girl?"

"That just shows you what I know." He reached to part the front of her robe and pull her on top of him, flattening her breasts almost painfully against his chest as they kissed. His hands roamed her back under the robe, making her breathless.

"Sometimes I used to watch you touching a horse and wish I were the horse," she said into his neck.

He laughed out loud, rolling her onto her side and leaning up on one elbow to see her face, which immediately began to flame. His expression told her she would regret that particular confession. She shut her eyes tightly. "Okay, *now* you've got to go. I'll never live that down."

"I've got to go, do I?" He put his hand over one breast, cupping and pressing, warm, then slid over to brush the other nipple lightly. He watched her face. "Are you sure you want me to go now?"

"Yes."

111

"That's a dangerous word." He didn't touch her again.

Her eyes were closed. Her eyelids felt heavy but she forced them open. "Is this a struggle for power?" She got to her elbow to his level and reached for his belt buckle. "Because I can do that too."

"So you can, but you don't need to. If you want me to leave, I will. Anytime."

"That sounds like a threat." Alex sat up fully and retrieved the cover of her opened robe, wrapping it tightly around her.

"I don't think it is. It's a statement of fact. I told you when I first met you that this was your show, boss lady, and it still is. Whatever attraction there is between us is a bonus. It doesn't alter the basics."

"No strings, you mean?"

"Something like that."

"Is that supposed to reassure me?"

He sighed deeply. "I don't know."

Alex leaned against him briefly. "I like it better when you don't talk," she said, pushing herself up from the bed. She walked to the end of the bed and leaned on the carved post. Rod carried his shoes past her, leaving a pat on her shoulder and a kiss on the side of her head.

When he was gone she dropped the robe on the floor and got into bed. She straightened the covers she didn't remember turning back and stretched out, a rigid form in the middle of the bed.

So much for the release of sexual pressure, she thought bitterly. They were worse off now than before. They were like two porcupines, prickly with defenses, who, unlike the porcupines in the joke, could make love with abandon, but who have to do everything else *very* carefully. But how could she continue to contend with him with any hope of maintaining her own tenuous position when in the very act of love she gave away her every advantage? All he had to do was touch her and she melted. He knew it too. But the touching solved nothing.

Alex didn't expect to sleep, but eventually she dozed as her mind gave in to her body, busy with memories of its own. As she stretched groggily toward morning, one question brought her abruptly awake. Had she said she loved him last night? She remembered thinking it, or feeling the thought pushing at the edges of her mind, but did she say it out loud? She hoped not. She didn't remember though, and the idea that it could have popped out in an unguarded moment galled her.

Thoroughly awake now and too angry and upset even to try for more sleep, she got up. The sun was already up, warming the world. The heat wave they had avoided for yesterday's show was evidently not to be put off further. She braided her hair tightly and pinned it up. She found her shorts and halter on the floor and decided defiantly to wear them, after a cool shower.

At the foot of the stairs she saw Rod's opened door and a glimpse of the shambles inside. She went on to the barn to begin clearing up the post-show clutter of left-behind clothing, tack, and even ribbons. It was going to be a long day.

The long day became a long, humid week, a week of flaring tempers and sharp words. Rod was merely distant; Alex was the one most out of sorts. She thought about Rod constantly, her emotions whipsawing between almost primal physical joy and despondent lethargy.

The weekend would bring another show, bigger and

more important. For the first time Rod was going to take his group of horses and advanced riders into what had been part of his own turf in Connecticut. Alex was taking her younger group to a local show.

By Friday Alex's nerves were stretched to the screaming point as Rod began loading horses for the trip, which would involve two nights away. She knew she was unreasonable, but she was convinced she would never see him again. He would never come back. Yet she did nothing to ease the tension between them. She called herself stubborn and stupid, but fear made her incapable of even smiling at Rod.

He had not gone yet when Cassie brought her some papers to sign. "Are you going to say a civil good-bye to Rod, or are you going to stay up here in the loft kicking over hay bales?"

Alex glared at her without answering because she didn't know the answer herself. She knew what she wanted to do, but not how to do it.

Cassie sighed and muttered something Alex only half heard.

"What did you say?"

Cassie looked at her directly. "I said, why don't you two just go to bed and get it over with so the rest of us can get on with our lives?"

Alex didn't know whether to laugh or cry, so she did both at once, with results that puzzled and alarmed Cassie. Despite the heat she folded Alex into her arms, easing her down to sit on the piled bales. As Alex gulped to a slowdown, she tried to talk. "It didn't *do* any good," she hiccuped, her erratic breathing making her accent the sentence oddly. "I'm such a mess."

114

Cassie grinned. "If sex didn't help, then there's nothing for it but to get married."

"Married?" The word seemed to choke Alex. "He doesn't even love me."

"Did he say so?"

"No. That's what I mean." She looked mournfully at Cassie. "He didn't say he loved me."

"Did he say he *didn't* love you?"

"He didn't say the word. Not once."

"Good. That means he does."

Alex just stared, big tears tracking the hay dust on her face.

Cassie laughed. "Really. The ones to watch out for are the ones who toss the word around like Frisbees. Or the ones who carefully explain they don't love you and they never will, they just like your body."

"*That* sounds like Rod."

"No. See, he's very honest and if he didn't love you, he'd tell you, but if he *did,* he'd be scared witless to say it. Just like he is."

"Or indifferent."

"Have you been looking at him this week?"

"Are you kidding? I can't even look in the mirror."

"Well, I've been looking at him and I can tell you he's got something weighty chewing on his insides. And he keeps looking at you when he thinks no one sees him."

"He's just thinking how he can't wait to get away from here and down to Connecticut."

"And that's what's eating you up." Cassie gave her a weary look. "Look, you've got to snap out of it and fix this up or one of those girls down there will renew old acquaintances over the weekend."

Alex's eyes grew round. "How did you know? Did he

115

tell you she's going to be there?"

"Who's *she*?"

"Diana Dunbar. He lived with her for a year."

"Oh. I didn't know. It was just a guess."

"Lucky guess."

"Will she be there?"

"I don't know. Probably."

Cassie got up from the hay bales and pulled Alex to her feet. "Wash your face and get a smile on and get down to the house. He went in to get some gear from his room."

"I can't go there."

"You can and you will."

Alex went to the ladder. The last she saw of Cassie as she descended the ladder was her encouraging smile. She splashed water on her face from the barrel and went to the house, wiping her hands on her shorts and trying to dry her face on grimy arms and the narrow shoulders of her tank top.

Rod's door was partly opened and she quailed indecisively until her fear of being discovered lurking outside his door overcame her terror of facing him. She knocked, opening the door wider in the process, to disclose Rod stuffing clothes into a canvas bag.

"Could you use a hand?" she asked, happy to say the first thing that came into her head. He straightened and watched her come closer. She couldn't read his expression, but she made hers purposeful, like a mother packing her son off to camp. As she reached to rescue a jumbled shirt he shut the suitcase, just missing her hands. She jumped back, staring.

"I'm a big boy, Alex. I can take care of my own clothes."

116

She ran her tongue over her lips. "Okay. Sorry." She looked longingly at the door.

"Why did you come here?"

"To say good-bye, to wish you luck."

"You could have yelled that from the barn door."

She stepped back, her temper flaring. "Okay, then, I will." She turned to leave, but he caught her arm and pulled her around against him.

"That's better," he laughed. "Get mad or something. I can't stand that whipped puppy look in your eyes."

"I'm not a whipped puppy and I don't give a damn where you go or—" He kissed her, and although she fought to hold on to her anger, it melted as if it had never been. He held her until she was limp, offering all the resistance of an overcooked noodle.

"Alex, you drive me crazy. I can't think straight. One minute I'm so mad at you I think if I get my hands on you again I'll wallop you within an inch of your life, then I *get* my hands on you and that's not what I want anymore."

He was demonstrating graphically his divided desires by the way he touched her. Alex backed away unsteadily. "Rod, I know. I'm awful. Just come back and we'll settle our differences somehow. I promise. I can't stand this either."

"Just come back?" He crossed his arms. "That's it, isn't it? You think I'm making my getaway now."

Alex opened his suitcase and picked up the shirt, folding it neatly and going on to smooth out other things. He took them from her, cramming them back inside.

"Don't avoid the issue, Alex."

"If you come back, then I'll know you'll come back."

"Until the next show."

"I'm going to that one too."

"If I didn't want to come back, it would take more than your presence to keep me in line."

"Will Diana be there?" It popped out.

"Now I *know* I'm going to smack you."

"Okay, okay. I'm sorry. I'm going. Good luck." She escaped and ran up to her room. She went to the bathroom for a drink and was appalled to see herself in the mirror. Her face was streaked with dirt, her eyes staring and red-rimmed. Just the image to send him back to cool, composed Diana in a hurry. She made repairs as best she could and joined the others to wave good-bye. She could read nothing special in his look, but Cassie claimed to be pleased.

The weekend, still hot and sticky, went by like a month in the hospital, to Alex a hideous reminder of how completely Rod had become central to her happiness. If he didn't come back, what would she do? And worse, if he *did* come back, what would she do?

He came back late Sunday night, bearing a clutch of ribbons, but in such a foul temper everyone gave him a wide berth. His car had overheated during the return, and he'd had to drive at a maddening crawl. It poured all day Monday, but Alex didn't see Rod until dinner. By then he had found out how much his car's repair would cost, so Alex ducked talking to him again.

When on Tuesday Rod disappeared after lunch and still was not back by supper, Alex decided to go for a solitary trail ride after supper, something she rarely had time for anymore. She had an enjoyable half hour to herself in the cool and blessedly drier evening air before Rod caught up with her. She was genuinely surprised to see him. The trail she had chosen from about four that looped her property was not well traveled.

"How did you find me?"

"Were you hiding?" He got off Freight Train, who had become his special mount, to join her on a favorite resting spot, a large flat granite outcropping.

She made a face. "You haven't seemed very happy since you came back."

"Which you read as regret that I came back, I suppose."

"No. You've had a bad time."

"Today I went shopping for a new car. Do you realize that since I've been here I've actually saved money?"

Alex laughed. "There's nothing to spend it on here."

"I found something today. I'd like you to see it tomorrow."

"I'd love to. I suppose you're going to keep it a surprise?" He cocked an eyebrow at her and she nodded. "I'll wait then." She leaned back against the rough stone and looked at him. "So how was Connecticut, really?"

"In your mouth the word becomes sinister," he commented, but he was smiling.

"I don't mean to be disapproving. It's not fair to ask a question in such a way that the person answering can't be honest."

"I'll be honest. It just amuses me." Preliminaries over, Rod leaned back and looked off at the grazing horses, considering his answer. "It was fine. The world has managed to keep spinning without me."

"That bad, huh?" Alex joked.

"I don't want to go back, Alex."

Something in his tone alarmed her. "But you will."

"For a couple of weeks, yes."

She waited. He looked at her, assessing her reaction.

"Someone I used to work with needs a couple of weeks, that's all, and he'll pay enough to make it worthwhile, and expenses, so all that drain is covered too."

"Diana Dunbar's father."

"Ed, his name is."

"Then you saw her."

"No, I didn't see her. She's no part of this."

Alex gave a laugh that was a snort of derision.

He shook his head. "Women." He looked to the sky in a gesture of supplication. "Why, dear God, do I keep getting involved with women?"

"Good question," she said crisply, getting to her feet.

"Alex." His voice stopped her cold. She looked back at him. "Sit down." She sat. "I'm trying very hard to keep my temper, but you're sending me straight up the wall."

Alex looked steadily at Rod, trying to keep her expression calm, but at the same time willing him to say what she wanted to hear.

"You have that *look* back again. You sit there like a little kid, hands folded in your lap like the first day of school."

"You told me to sit."

He turned away. "Ah, what's the use? I try to live my life doing what I know how to do, doing the best I can, trying to be fair. Even with women I try to be fair."

"Even with women? How decent of you."

"Alex, damn it . . ."

"All right. You feel aggrieved. Well, so do I. It's what I thought would happen, what you told me wouldn't—"

"It's only two weeks."

"Is it? Word of the man who said he wouldn't go back?"

"I said I wouldn't *leave*. And I won't. I'll come back.

120

I suppose it isn't fair and you have a beef, but really, Alex, it's so much money."

"Why is it so much money? Have you thought of that?"

"What do you mean?"

"I mean, Daddy Dunbar is buying another chance for his daughter with you."

"Oh, Alex, for heaven's sake, that's crazy."

"Think about it. Is there something only you can do for him? I mean with the horses?"

"I do make my living that way."

"Of course you do. I'm not belittling what you do. But doesn't it strike you as even a bit contrived that you're needed so desperately?"

"No."

"And you really believe Diana has nothing to do with this?"

"She doesn't to me."

"Ah. Small difference. Then her name came up?"

"Well, of course it did. I asked about her. It would have been rude not to. She's not dead."

"Not married either, I bet."

"So what?"

"I rest my case."

"You don't have a case."

"No. You're right, I don't. I went into this knowing what would happen, so how can I act surprised that it's happened?"

She started to get up again; this time Rod put his hand on her arm. "Will you listen to me? Please?" She stayed still.

He took his hand away and reached for a small branch of an overhanging tree. It didn't break easily, but he worked it back and forth until it came off.

"You asked me about Connecticut, meaning all that show biz? I don't like it now. I really don't. I missed you. I missed Ellen and Miriam, Cassie even." He began stripping leaves from the length of the twig, concentrating on the task, but playing with it, not looking at Alex.

"Thanks for telling me that. We missed you."

"I suppose our discussion about us has to wait now?"

"About us?"

"About you upstairs and me downstairs? About you driving me nuts?"

"What is there to discuss? Our attempt at anything else didn't seem to help."

"I wasn't complaining."

"You said I make you mad and it seems to be true." She looked at him bleakly. "As bodies together we seem to be fine, but as people we have a lot of problems I guess."

"Do we? Maybe if we just let the bodies take over for a while, the people would take care of themselves."

Alex laughed and got up. "Nice try, Rod, but I can't afford your stud fee."

The remark was lightly offered, tossed over her shoulder as she turned from Rod to climb down from the rock. It was not lightly received, however. Because she wasn't looking at him, Alex missed seeing the sequence of surprise, hurt, and anger that overtook Rod and would have sent her scrambling out of his reach. Instead, he caught her in mid-climb, one foot on the rock, the other almost on the ground, and hauled her back bodily to face him. Too surprised to offer any resistance, which would have been useless anyway, Alex stared mutely into his furious eyes, a rag doll in his hands. He started to shake her limp form, her feet flailing uselessly beneath her. "Damn you!"

He let her go then as suddenly as he had caught her, and

she reeled as she regained her feet on the ground. He steadied her automatically, his face a blank mask of anger. She edged away from him to the other side of the rock and leaned there to catch her breath and regain her senses. She looked at his flinty dark profile, his mouth a tight slash grimly outlined by his moustache.

"That didn't help any either, did it?" she asked.

He looked at her flushed face, his eyes full of pain. "No."

"Would it help if I said I'm sorry? I didn't mean that the way it sounded."

He looked away.

She sighed. "No, I didn't think so. But I am sorry. I love you, Rod. I've loved you since the night we met, but I don't know how to live with it. I've tried not to show my feelings because I know it's hopeless and all I do is muddy the water around us. I'm sorry."

She turned away and untied her horse from the tree to climb on stiffly. She didn't look at Rod but she could see him anyway, the hulking embodiment of hurt anger, half sitting on the rock, his arms characteristically clutched over his chest.

The ride home was as painful mentally as it was physically disorienting, but she wouldn't have minded any of it if it had only helped someone. As it was, Rod only felt worse for attacking her, and she felt worse for confessing her love. They were hopeless together and although Alex knew she would be worse alone, now she knew she had already driven him away with her jealousy. That she was right was no comfort.

She put Greenbriar in his stall and wandered aimlessly in the barn for so long, she had to hide behind a door when

Rod came back. He put Freight Train away and stood for a time in the open barn door, a broad-shouldered silhouette against the evening light. He looked toward the house, then walked to his car and drove away. She waited till the sound of his motor died away before she went to her rooms.

CHAPTER FIVE

When Alex woke the next morning the muggy heat was back, but Rod wasn't. She wasn't surprised, yet it did add another jog of pain. She didn't see him return, but by afternoon she heard his piercing whistle as he signaled one of his riders from the sidelines of the ring. As always, one part of her mind dwelt obsessively on him while the rest of her tried to ignore all thought of yesterday, so she was disproportionately startled when he reached to take a pail of water from her hand late in the afternoon as she was turning from the water barrel. For his chivalry he got most of the contents of the bucket poured into his left boot.

He squished on to deliver the rest of the water for her before he turned to look at her. She was near tears. "It's all right, Alex. It's just a boot. I have two other pairs. It felt cool besides."

"If only you didn't sneak up on me." She stood blinking in the middle of the barn floor.

He took her arm and pulled her to the side as Steve

125

brought the two Clydesdales through the barn to hitch them to the hay wagon. She watched the massive horses pass, then started away. "I'll get your boots."

He held her arm. "I'll get my own boots. Later. I wanted to ask a favor of you." Bewildered, Alex stared up at Rod.

He sighed wearily at her expression and she turned away.

"I wouldn't bother you with this if I could think of anyone else to help me."

She closed her eyes. "I deserve that. Ask away."

"I stayed over at Henry's last night," he began. "They're away—"

"You don't have to explain anything to me," she interrupted.

"Damn it, Alex, I'll throw you headfirst in that barrel if you don't shut up."

She shut her mouth firmly. How long had it been since he'd said anything that didn't begin with 'Damn it, Alex'?

"What I want you to do is help me get Ellen over to Henry's for a swim tonight. She'll go, I know, and getting her there is no problem, but she probably doesn't have a bathing suit. Could you fix her up?"

Alex was stunned. "What a great idea."

"Do you have an extra suit?"

"Of course. She used to swim well. She'll be so happy."

"You come too, please?"

She frowned, wondering if Ellen wouldn't rather have Rod to herself.

"She might need help I couldn't give her without embarrassing her, Alex."

"Sure, yeah, you're right. Did you tell her yet?"

"I wanted to check with you first. I'm taking her to the

house in a few minutes and I'll see what she thinks." He turned away and Alex reached for his arm impulsively.

"Rod. You're a good man. Thank you." There was a flash of pain in his eyes before he turned away again.

At supper Ellen was so excited she couldn't eat. Her joy was contagious, bringing back some of the spirit Alex and Rod had leached from the group with their troubled relationship. She tried on two bathing suits before deciding on one and giving herself up to be carried to the car. Because she was so light, Rod suggested leaving the chair behind.

Only when they were outside did Alex remember Rod's new car, a gleaming Audi into which he tucked Ellen with a kiss. Alex climbed into the back seat with Ellen's bag of clothes for the return trip, remembering that she could have gone with Rod to bring the car home but for her stupidity. Using the excuse of showing off his new car, Rod gave Ellen a leisurely drive through Concord before stopping at Henry's back entrance.

The pool was small, a glorified bathtub set into the ground amidst so many plantings it appeared the Chandlers were trying to hide it, but the water looked refreshingly cool. Rod placed Ellen on a lounger and went inside to do his housecheck, enabling Alex to help Ellen prepare for her plunge. Alex saw that she was near tears and had to struggle to contain her own emotions, but by the time Rod appeared in his suit Ellen had regained her usual wisecracking demeanor.

Alex wore the other one-piece suit, the one Ellen had rejected, and sat on the edge to watch as Rod carried her into the water. They soon discovered that Ellen needed little assistance after the bouyant water took over. Although her legs could not support her weight, she could move them, and with her nearly normal right arm she could execute a functional sidestroke that got her handily from one side of the pool to the other.

In the ecstacy of freedom and motion, Ellen sang and laughed until she grew tired. Then she insisted they swim while she rested on the lounge chair. She goaded them into racing, ordering Rod to swim one-armed so Alex could win, then asked for one last paddle before they went home. On the way back Rod stopped to buy them all ice cream cones, and when they turned Ellen over to Miriam, she was delirious with satisfaction.

After Miriam shooed her away from their quarters, Alex went to climb the stairs to her rooms, but found Rod sitting on the second step. "Come back to Henry's with me," he said.

She held up her bundle of wet things and said, "Let me trade these and get my other suit."

He nodded and kissed the back of the hand that dangled near his face. She went to the bathroom and stuffed her wet things into the hamper. She brought a beach robe and another change of shorts as well as the suit and some hair fixings and rejoined Rod, who hadn't moved.

"I like your car," she said as he got in beside her. "It looks like you."

He patted the gear box. "It's still in the way."

She didn't say anything while they drove, as her thoughts rattled between Ellen's moment of happiness and her nervousness at being with Rod.

He carried her tote bag, putting it on the table by the pool. "Show me the suit," he ordered.

She took the bag and circled around him. "Trust me. You'll like it."

He had two glasses of wine poured when she came out wearing the most daring suit she'd ever owned. It was golden brown, the most flattering color for her tawny skin, and tied in four places, at the sides of the hips, the neck, and the back. Even with the ties triple-checked Alex felt insecure because between the ties was a minimum of cloth.

"You're right. I do like it," he said, handing her a glass.

"I bought it last year at the beginning of the summer, but I never dared wear it." She took a big swallow of wine. "Where did Eliza and Henry go?"

"To the Cape."

"That's right. They have a place there." She would soon be babbling; her nerves were already stretched beyond endurance. She took another swallow of her drink, then put the glass down firmly. "I'm going in the water now while I'm still partially in control of my senses." She stood up resolutely, then sat down again quickly as she realized how standing like that next to him displayed her body. She began to undo her hair, but he reached across the table to stop her.

"Let me." He came around the table and gently pulled her to her feet beside him. First he kissed her neck, then he began to unpin her coil of hair. It was already wet, so it fell heavily onto a shoulder. She unwound it, finding the pins he had missed, and shook it a bit to free it around her neck. He was still standing so close beside her, any move would put her in his arms. He patted her hair. "I'm a sucker for long hair," he laughed, reaching for her.

"If you kiss me again, I'll drown when I get in the pool."

"Then I could rescue you." He kissed her without letting their bodies touch. She backed into the table, then edged away.

"If I'm not afraid to get my hair wet; why should you stay out?"

"To watch you."

She held out her hand. "Come with me."

He took her hand. At the edge of the pool she noticed his unaware stance and instinctively she seized the opportunity to avenge her dunking in the water barrel. With demurely downcast eyes that completely hid her intent, she executed a quick trip-and-push maneuver that dumped him, totally off-guard, into the water with a pool-emptying splash. She had several seconds to gloat at the side of the pool as he took his time coming to the surface.

"I told you I'd get even," she crowed, twirling in delight. It took only one glance, however, at the look in his eyes as he came to the edge again to squash her glee. In her heady moment of triumph she had forgotten completely the second part of her plan for revenge, escape. She had caught him napping, but he was far from unconscious now. She backed away as he hoisted himself out, dripping. His grin did absolutely nothing to reassure her. Never in her life had she seen a more menacing smile.

While she backed up she sorted through her options. She'd never beat him to the house or the car. She was a dead duck where she was because he was going to spank her. She knew it as surely as she knew her name, from the way he hitched at his bathing suit, from the gleam in his eye, and from his grin. Even though she knew he would not really hurt her, she had no intention of suffering through the indignity he clearly planned, and certainly not while wearing this scrap of a bathing suit.

She bought a few seconds by sweetly pleading for mercy while she edged behind a chair. "Rod, please. Now we're even. Fair's fair, okay?"

She feigned a move away from the pool, keeping the chair between them. When she could see he was certain he could grab her anytime he wanted, she made her real move—a headlong dash for the safety of the water.

She came up to the surface, weak with relief. She would stay in the water until she turned into a prune, happy in the knowledge that it was physically impossible for him to spank her as long as she was submerged. She was careful not to look triumphant as she paddled around at his feet. He looked amused and she was only slightly apprehensive as he sat on the edge and slipped back into the water. She swam toward him, smiling sweetly.

"Think you're pretty cute, don't you?" His grin had returned as he backstroked away from her. "But I can wait, too, you know. You can't spend your life underwater."

"I'll worry about that tomorrow," she laughed.

"I'd worry about it tonight if I were you."

"Maybe I can distract you," she teased, swimming beside him so that her hair trailed near his face. He caught a handful of it and pulled her up short to kiss her.

"Maybe you can at that."

She swam away but he caught her ankle and brought her back. He was as omnipresent as the water, bumping against her like a large insistent dolphin determined to play. It was several minutes before she realized his randomness was giving way to a deliberate assault on the ties of her bathing suit. With four of them to defend she was kept busy. While she was occupied with the bottoms, he swam behind her and undid the tie at the back of her neck. As she tried to corral those drifting strings, he finished off the one at her back and pulled the top away. She swam away with him at her heels. She reached the edge and clung there, facing it. He reached around her to fit his hands over her breasts. "I did ask you to go skinny-dipping with me."

"Revenge has many forms?" she asked.

"This isn't revenge," he said, his thumbs rubbing her taut nipples. "Does that feel like revenge?"

Alex hung from the side of the pool, helpless and breathless as one hand slid down over her midriff to untie the side of her bikini bottom. He pulled on the back section, his hand curving over the side of her hip. The other hand followed the same course, the water adding a debilitating sensuousness to his touch. She couldn't have stopped him if she had wanted to, and she no longer wanted to. The front and back sections of her bikini bottoms floated down and he pulled them free. Still she clung to the side, her shoulder to his face.

"I thought you wanted to swim?" He nudged her head with his, pressing against her back, his hands holding her hips in place.

"I can't swim now."

His hand stroked over her bottom. "Want to get out?"

"No." She tried to move away along the edge of the pool.

He laughed, following.

"Rod, a car just came into the driveway."

He looked up to see headlights through the slatted board fence. He pulled himself out onto the edge of the pool as a flashlight bobbed at the unlocked gate. The pool itself was lit by low edge bulbs that diffused light through the luminous water, and the surrounding pool area had low indirect lights with a few spots directed at the plantings, but the driveway and gate were dark.

The gate swung open. "Police here," said a voice behind

the flashlight. Rod stood up and the light went out as a uniformed man approached the pool. Alex sunk lower.

"Neighbors called that the owners were away and there were people around."

Rod walked to him. "I'm Rod Gilbert. Henry asked me to keep an eye on the house. Said to use the pool if it got warm."

"That your car?"

"Yes. I just bought it today. I work at Sunny Meadow Farm." He gestured to Alex's head. "Alex Baxter. She owns the farm. We're old friends of the Chandlers."

"What's his wife's name?"

"Eliza. They went to the Cape for two weeks. They have a place at Barnstable. They'll be back Sunday." Rod tried to keep the officer from getting too close to the pool. "Do you want to see my license?" He gestured to his clothes across the pool, indicating willingness to get them.

"No. That's okay. Just checking. Enjoy your swim. It looks like fun." He went out the gate with a final lingering glance back at the pool. As Rod turned back he saw the top of Alex's bikini, two brown triangles with attached strings, floating in the center of the glowing water. When the car was gone he gave himself over to hoots of laughter that Alex watched in stony disapproval.

"Why didn't you invite him in for a swim?"

Rod dove out into the water to where her bathing suit top drifted and brought it back to her. "He couldn't see you," he assured her, "but he sure as hell wanted to." He fetched the rest of her suit and placed it on the concrete. "Poor guy was bug-eyed," he laughed. He grabbed Alex by the sides of her waist and tugged backward to break her grip on the pool. It wasn't hard to do because her hands were cramped from clutching the side for so long. As they

133

floated backward, his hands caressed any part of her he could reach.

"Two seconds later and I wouldn't have been able to climb out either," Rod said, circling her, undoing the belt of his bathing suit. While he was busy, Alex swam away, out of his reach. Even without his persistent and arousing touch the feeling of being naked in the water was delicious. She dove deep underwater and let herself rise slowly, turning in disorienting coils. She broke the surface of the water next to Rod and swam back a few strokes.

"I love to watch your backstroke," he said.

She took another deep breath and submerged again, but this time he caught her and kissed her mouth as they rose together, her long hair fanning out around them. She laughed as she caught her breath. "Do you know I've never been swimming without clothes before?"

"That's a waste. You look like a mermaid." He swam closer. "I've never made love underwater."

"Rod," she squeaked.

"Unless you want to get out, that's what's going to happen. I can't watch you much longer."

"Then close your eyes," she said haughtily.

"It doesn't help. My imagination is too good." He maneuvered her to the edge of the pool, backing her against the side. He wedged her with his knee and kissed her, pulling her up so her head was above water. She had to cling to his shoulders as he lifted her against him, one hand spread over her buttocks. She began to tremble, and when he took his mouth from hers her teeth chattered.

"Come on, you're getting chilled. Out."

She shook her head. "I'm not cold."

"You're cold. Listen to your teeth."

"I'm just . . ."

"Just what?"

She swallowed. "Excited."

He smiled. "Sounds good, but what you really are is scared."

"No, I'm not." Her teeth rattled noisily.

His smile widened to a knowing grin. "Sure you are, and for good reason." He kissed her nose. "Because I have a bone to pick with you."

Her last reserves of strength ebbed away. "Rod." It was a whisper.

He climbed out and got a towel before he reached for her hand to pull her out. He wrapped her shaking body in the towel and with an end patted her face dry. He wrapped another towel around himself and picked up their suits. She began to walk toward the house, using tiny, and she hoped, unobtrusive steps. He put the suits on the table and picked up the wine and the two glasses to follow her.

"Move it along, Alex. You weren't going to get away anyway, so open up the door for me."

She looked at the room they entered. "Upstairs," he gestured with his head.

"My clothes are in the bathroom down there."

"You don't need your clothes. I have a robe in my room you can have."

She went where he directed, concentrating on keeping the towel out from under her feet on the stairs. His room featured a large brass bed and several handsome chests. From the glow of lights outside she could tell that the two tall windows looked out on the pool. Rod put the wine down on the table by the bed and ripped back the bedcovers. Alex stood, shivering still but not chattering, in the middle of the floor. He went into the adjoining bathroom and when he came out he was dry and wrapped around the waist by a smaller towel. He tossed her another towel and brought a blow dryer to the bed, plugging it into a bedside socket.

"Drink some wine and I'll help you get dry." She started to sit down on the bed. "You can have the robe if you'd rather." He handed her a huge plaid robe and nodded to the bathroom. She finished drying there and rubbed her hair with the towel before going out in the robe.

She took the wine and sat on the edge of the bed. He directed the nozzle at her hair, lifting and tossing sections of the soaked hair to expose it to the heat.

"Are you sure you're not a hairdresser?" she asked. He put such a blast of hot air down the front of the robe that the cloth blew back. "Guess not," she laughed. "No one's ever done that to me in a salon."

"Their loss."

He worked on, drinking occasionally from his glass, telling her to turn, while she did as he said, drinking now and then. When he shut off the dryer her hair wasn't dry but merely damp. "When you look in the mirror you'll know I'm no hairdresser. Do you want a comb or brush?"

"Both." She knelt on the bed as he brought an old-fashioned bedroom set of comb, brush, and hand mirror from the bureau. She laughed at her reflection and took up the comb to work out some of the tangles. "I haven't seen a set like this since my grandmother's time. She used to let me play house with it."

Rod watched her, his expression both fond and teasing as a smile played around his mouth, lifting the corners of his moustache. She reached for the hairbrush but he held it out of her reach, grinning now, the gleam back in his eyes. "Turn around."

She looked at the hairbrush in his hand. He wouldn't. "Rod. Don't you dare," She hitched back on the bed awkwardly.

With one arm he reached to pull her close, still holding the flat-backed brush out of her reach. He tucked her back against his side, his face in her neck. "What do you think I'm going to do? Paddle you?" he laughed. "I'm glad to know you recognize what you deserve, but that's not what I have in mind." He propped her up and began to brush her hair as she would have done herself. Calmer, but still wary, she watched him kneeling beside her, his powerful chest and shoulder muscles contracting and releasing with every slight motion of his arms.

When her hair was smooth he put the tools of the hairdressing trade on the table. "Do you have any idea how much fun it is to tease you? Your eyes get perfectly round with fright."

She reached for her wine with a toss of her hair. "You can be pretty scary. And I'm not totally crazy. You *were* going to spank me when you got out of the pool. It was written all over you. I can read body language too."

"You're damn right I was going to spank you. I'm still going to do it, too, but not tonight. Tonight I'm going to love you, just love you till your bones ache." His eyes were almost black with intensity. Alex closed her eyes and swallowed hard. "But if you insist on talking about how you feel, about anything," he went on, his voice stern, "then I swear I'll put you across my knee and wear out my hand on your backside. Do you understand?"

She nodded and he took her glass away and turned out the light. Even in the sudden darkness his hand unerringly went to the opening of her outsize robe as he reached for her, half kneeling on the bed. As he tugged the robe apart

137

to cover her breast with his warm hand, she didn't move, but not because she felt passive or uninvolved. Her stillness enabled her to savor the intensity of her feelings, to concentrate totally on Rod.

He pushed the robe off her shoulders, stroking her smooth hair and the skin of her shoulders and arms, seeking a response from her mouth as he kissed her. She opened her mouth obediently to his tongue, but still held back, still preserving the exquisite painfulness of distance between them. Sensing a barrier, Rod redoubled his efforts to gain her response, concentrating on her breasts, seeking with his hands and mouth to remove her apparent resistance.

Just when she could pretend no longer, he pulled back to look at her in the faint light from outside. "Are you scared of me? Or mad at me?" he demanded. Then, catching a revealing expression on her face, his voice changed again. "Or are you teasing me? Because if you are . . ."

She stopped him with a kiss that more than answered his question, leaping the self-constructed barriers. His passion flared like paper touched with flame.

"Alex, you are the most maddening woman."

"Shh." She kissed him lightly, shrugging the robe off her arms. The belt of the robe still kept the lower half of her body swathed in plaid cloth but her breast pressed his bare chest as she reached up to put her arms around his shoulders. She arched backward, holding on tightly, so that only the tips of her breasts grazed against him. She moved from side to side, letting his hands on her back support her languorous weight.

"Alex, oh, Alex."

She smiled up at him dreamily. "Whose bones ache now?"

He lowered her to her back and pulled away the robe to touch her deeply. "Yours do. Tell me they do."

"I'm not supposed to talk," she managed breathlessly.

"I'm making an exception. Just . . . this . . . once."

"Oh, yes, yes. Oh, Rod, yes."

Then she was beyond words as he swept away his towel wrap and covered her with the hard male length of his body. She felt the impact of his heated skin in every cell of her being. Logic might have suggested that after his playfulness in the pool, further seduction was unneeded, but Rod wasn't being logical, nor was Alex.

He held her head between his hands, most of his weight on his elbows, and brushed soft kisses over her cheeks, eyes, nose, and chin. She tried to turn her mouth to meet his, but he didn't allow it. Even when she took his head in her hands she couldn't bring his lips nearer than the corner of her mouth or keep him from tracing her lips with the tip of his tongue. Only when she began to chase his tongue with her own did he relent, taking possession of her mouth with satisfying completeness. His tongue continued to play with hers in a sensuous imitation of conquest and retreat. Alex wove her fingers into the brushy softness of his dark hair and let her thumbs stroke the edges of his ears.

When it seemed he would never let her move, never let her breathe freely, she brought her knees up on either side of his legs to rub the sides of his calves with the soles of her feet. The action cradled his weight intimately against the center of her body, making her invitation explicit. He lifted his head and smiled. "Oh, Alex, you feel so warm and good."

She couldn't keep from smiling back any more than she could contain her mixed reaction as he rolled to his side, taking her with him in a way that compensated her for the loss of his closeness by the attention of his hands and lips to her breasts. With a tender, feathering touch he circled the aching centers until she writhed with impatient demand that he finally rewarded by taking one nipple deeply into the heat of his mouth. Her incoherent cry of pleasure sent him on a passionate journey of discovery down the length of her body.

Within her heated skin Alex could only bite back the words of love she knew he didn't want to hear. But the words sang in her veins, no less eloquent for being unspoken. She could no more stop loving him than she could control her racing pulse or keep her hands from reaching out to stroke the wide bands of muscles under his skin.

Rod moved to accommodate her tentative exploration, urging her, "Oh, yes, touch me, please."

Startled to have drawn his attention, Alex drew back, hesitant. He took her hands to his mouth and kissed the palms. "This is lesson two, Alex. I want to be touched just the way you do. Your hands feel soft and warm. I need that."

There was a hunger in his dark eyes that made it easy to overcome her self-consciousness. The springy tuft of his chest hair felt both familiar and exotic to her playing fingers. She let his eyes and his response guide her, heady with the thought that he felt the same ache that blossomed within her. She stroked down to his navel, but as she tried to retreat he took her hand and held it against him. "Don't tease, Alex."

Her expression told him she had intended to, but the desire, the sheer naked need thickening his voice, made

140

her relent. Then she was aided by instincts old as time as she sought to please him, expressing with her hands and mouth the love she felt for this man.

Gentle hands under her arms lifted her back to his side and nestled her there with tender, loving touches. His big hands were worshipful, reverent, as he brought her again to the very edge of fulfillment, filling her body, mind, and spirit with himself. With love-dazed eyes she saw that his need equaled hers. His eyes glowed with more than passion, and as he possessed her with stunning completeness, hope soared within her, keeping pace with their consuming passion. Hope of winning his love bound Alex to Rod as surely as the heat of their joined bodies welded them together.

Long after she felt the hammered beat of Rod's heart slow and become steady under her cheek, Alex was too content to move or even to notice that her hair was tangled under his arm. Finally, though, she stirred and tried to lift her head from his damp chest. When his hand pushed her back down, she complained, "Rod, you've got my hair caught."

"Good. Don't move."

She tried again with the same results, so she poked his ribs with a sharp finger. His startled reaction was a good deal more than she bargained for, but it did release her hair from under his upper arm. It also got her pinned to the bed under one arm and leg.

He kissed a corner of her mouth and subjected her to an amused but leisurely appraisal. "Do I have to resort to chains as well as a gag to keep you in line?"

"Idle threats," she scoffed.

"Don't you wish."

"Just a typical macho male."

"Listen to the woman of the world. Tell me what you know about macho males, boss lady."

"I'm being invited to talk?"

"No." He kissed her. "You're invited to lie there in helpless adoration. We macho males are very big on helpless adoration."

"I've noticed." She kissed him lightly. "It's not one of my major talents though."

"Practice makes perfect." He turned to his side and groped for a sheet, pulling her back against his chest spoon-fashion, his knees behind hers. "Go to sleep."

"We have to go home. *I* have to go home."

"Later. I want to sleep with you."

She tried to stir but he tightened the hold of his arm across her body and she gave up. Giving up was getting easier and easier, she mused, nestling into him. Did that mean he was right, or that her character was weak? The answer eluded her but sleep did not.

She woke up when Rod, freshly showered and shaved, sat down beside her. "Only the pure of heart sleep so soundly," he commented, watching her eyes start to open slowly, then fly open in dismay. Bright morning sunshine drenched the bed.

She sat up quickly, then grabbed the sheet to her chest. She glared up at his smile. "Stop laughing at me. It's not funny."

"Sure it is." He smoothed back her hair and put the robe in her lap. "I brought up your bag and all your things. The bathroom is all yours."

What was all hers was a steambath, swampy with Rod's huge wet footprints and dropped wet towels. Nevertheless, the shower refreshed her, and with fresh clothes to put on she could face even the lateness of the hour of their return

142

to the farm. She did her best to mop up the bathroom, hanging towels on every available bar to dry.

"We can always pretend we went somewhere very early this morning and we're just getting back now," Alex said as she repacked her bag.

He laughed. "What would your father have thought of his little girl?"

She frowned. "He'd have locked me in my room and thrown away the key."

"Then I could rescue you."

"You seem to have this thing about rescuing me." It was her turn to be amused.

"I have a lot of 'things' about you." His look was enigmatic.

She smiled. "Good." She stretched up to kiss him, accepting his proprietary pat on the fanny without bristling at all.

Maybe he was right. Maybe all she had to do was shut up and everything would fall into place. Anyway, at least she'd tried it his way, so if he didn't come back from New York, she wouldn't have to reproach herself for stubbornness.

At the farm she left her tote bag in his car and got out as if they had just been on an innocent breakfast date, following Rod's succinct advice; never apologize, never explain. If they were missed in the tumult of show preparations, most of the crew were too busy to comment just then. Yet later, when Cassie was leaving for home, she said with elaborate casualness, "Alex, since Gerald's coming with us this weekend, why don't you ride down with Rod and let one of us drive your car?"

She frowned. "Gee, Cassie, I don't think that's—"

"That's a great idea, Cassie," Rod's deep voice overrode

her from behind. "Thanks. We'll do that." He went by them both out the door without a glance at Alex who, although pleased, opened her mouth to protest. Cassie shook her head in mock despair and left too. Alex turned back, meeting the same expression from Ellen and Miriam.

"Oh, all right!" Alex thumped up to her room to escape. She knew they were right, but being managed all the time was getting tiresome. She was nervous about the weekend and catatonic about the following two weeks when Rod would be at the Dunbars'. At times like this it seemed suspense was worse than any outcome, however horrible.

The next day, departure day, was such a blur of activity Alex hadn't even finished packing when Rod bounded up the stairs to bring down her bag. He found her near tears, indecisively holding two dresses over her opened suitcase.

"You're going to a horse show, Alex. You don't need either of those."

She rounded on him. "You just stay out of this, Rod. I don't need you to tell me what to wear."

He took them out of her hands. "Sure you do. Show me what you have in there and I'll tell you whether it's right or not."

"Rod . . ."

When she didn't show him, he began to rummage through her bag, holding up garments, making two piles of them. "You need one dress and an extra pair of pants besides your riding stuff. That's all." He patted one pile. "There."

Speechless with indignation, Alex started to draw back her arm to hit him, tears forgotten in fury. He took her arm in one hand and pulled her against him with the other, utterly unperturbed. He kissed her nose and turned

144

to latch the suitcase, lifting it down. "Hang up those things and get a wiggle on. We need to be going."

"I hate you," she said childishly.

He went out. "Be downstairs in two minutes or I'll leave without you."

When she got into the car, still red-faced, he said nothing until they were zooming on the highway. Then he said, "You're really cute when you get mad, you know that? You're just like those kittens at the barn when they get wet."

She glared at him, then looked away as he laughed. "Makes me want to pick you up by the scruff of the neck and stroke your fur." She put her fingers into her ears and stared straight ahead, blocking out anything more that he could say, but not the image of herself he found so amusing. It didn't help her confidence that he saw her that way and that he knew she was no more effective against him than a kitten, wet or dry.

For the rest of the trip he went out of his way to ease her nervous anticipation, amusing her with stories of disastrous shows he'd attended. She decided, looking at his profile, that even if he was a bit of a bully at times, his intentions were good. She admired him; she trusted him; she loved him. She didn't believe she would win him, however, and her heart ached to think of life without him.

When he looked her way she turned quickly to stare out the window, sure he could easily read the love in her expression. "Going to sleep with me tonight, beautiful?" His tone was light, but the words poured over her like melted butter.

"Rod, you know better than . . ."

He just laughed and slapped the side of her thigh.

At the showgrounds they went their separate ways,

145

each caring for a different group of riders. Rod supervised stabling the horses, with assistance from Cassie and two grooms who were to sleep on cots set up in the stable area. Gerald took charge of Alex's younger riders, seeing them installed in their motel rooms, rounding them up for meals, and taking care of their non-show-related problems, while Alex registered them for their classes and got their numbers. Even with every gear smoothly engaged, problems continually cropped up to be dealt with throughout the weekend—lost money, misplaced clothing, a lame horse, canceled classes.

By Saturday night Alex was frayed, physically and mentally. She had reprimanded two squabbling girls, chased away a stray dog from nipping the legs of one of the horses, and was ready to go back to the motel for a shower and something more substantial than showground hot dogs, when an excited voice several paces behind her stopped her cold in her tracks.

"Dee Dee!" the voice screeched. "Wait up."

Alex whirled around in time to see a tall, cool-looking blonde turn back to wait for the plump matron who had hailed her. Both wore the finest riding clothes, but Diana Dunbar had the inherent style and figure to make rags look like couturier fashions. Her bare arms were tanned, her legs long and lean, her hips nonexistent, and her hair was a pale cap that even a tornado couldn't dishevel.

Alex faded sideways off the path between tents, bending as if she had something in her boot so she could watch Diana unobtrusively as she briefly bore the older woman's gushing attentions. When she turned back to stalk the path to Sunny Meadow Farm's stabling area, Alex continued to watch, huddling, sweaty and miserable.

After Diana was gone from sight Alex stood up, but

instead of going along the same path to where Rod was finishing up, waiting to give her a ride back to the motel, she stumbled off to the side in pursuit of oblivion. She had absolutely no intention of coming upon Rod's reunion with Diana, however tired she was. She would give Diana time to get Rod and leave, then she would go back for her gear and find another ride to the motel, even if she had to hitchhike.

Their area was at the outskirts of the encampment, so Alex could waste a bit of time circling other stables before she had to head back. Because her eyes were blurred by unsheddable tears, she stepped, with disastrous consequences to her boots, into a pile of fresh manure, and by the time she got to the stable she knew she would howl if she saw anyone she knew, so she sneaked into the tack area by the side. She rummaged in her purse for something to wipe her face, found her compact, and began to clean up. When she checked her hair in the compact mirror, trying to tuck up the sagging wisps of escaped, damp hair around her face, she caught part of Rod's glowering face in the tiny glass. She dropped the compact and burst into tears.

He remained a silent hulk at her shoulder until she sobbed to a halt, then he bent to pick up her compact. She turned around slowly, wiping her eyes on the back of her hand, looking behind him for Diana.

"I thought you'd be gone," she said, trying out her voice.

"Why did you sneak in here?"

"I didn't want to see anyone."

"I was waiting for you."

"You didn't have to. I was going to get another ride."

147

"Something wrong with my car?" His voice had a dangerous edge.

She turned away, her shoulders sagging. "I figured it would be crowded."

"Why don't you explain that." His arms were folded over his chest.

She walked past him to look into the unpeopled stable center between stalls. "She left?"

"Who left?"

"Don't be so cute, Rod. You know who. Diana." Her voice curdled the name. "And don't pretend you didn't see her, because I saw her marching straight for this tent."

"That was forty-five minutes ago. Where have you been since then?"

"None of your business." The childish taunt was out before she could stop it, but when she saw the flare of anger in Rod's eyes she hastily added, "Around." It wasn't much of an improvement, but it did seem to defuse, temporarily, his exasperation.

"So you saw Diana coming this way and you decided she was meeting me and that I'd leave without a word to you when I'd told you I'd wait for you. You put great stock in my word, don't you?"

"It wasn't any big deal. I told you I knew I could get a ride."

"No one in his right mind would give you a ride in those boots."

"I can clean them up. I was going to now."

"Don't let me stop you."

She went to the side of the tent and out to drag her boot in the high grass, then returned to take it off with a boot jack. He took it from her and carried it away. She stood on one foot, then hobbled to sit until he returned.

"Why didn't you go with her?" She put on the cleaned boot.

"What makes you think I was asked? Couldn't she have just come to say hello?"

"No. She didn't look like that."

He laughed at her expression.

"You don't owe me anything, Rod. Not even to finish out the season. We got along just fine before you came and we'll get along just fine after you leave."

His face hardened and he turned away abruptly. "Good. I'll remember that."

Alex had to trot to keep up with him on the way to the car, and although she knew he was hurt now as well as annoyed, she could think of no way to bridge the chasm between them. She wanted him to choose her, but not out of duty or a sense of obligation. If her words had been harsh, at least they had been clear. He knew she loved him; she'd told him that in every way there was to convey the message. Now it was up to him.

CHAPTER SIX

Alex took a long time over her shower once Rod delivered her back to the motel. He had extended no dinner invitation—not that she expected him to—so she made do with vending-machine food—stale crackers and cheese, a candy bar, and coffee. On her way back to her room from the motel lobby she saw Rod, handsomely suited, get in his car and drive away. She made it to her room before she burst into tears, and by the time she got to her coffee after her cry, it was cold. She drank it anyway. That was another mistake. She needed to sleep, if only to get away from the tiresomeness of her self-recriminations, but after the coffee hit her overwrought stomach, nothing could persuade her eyes to close.

She looked a wreck the next day. Rod also looked terrible, but that was caused by overindulgence rather than misery, as more than one person pointed out to her. Cassie tried to be sympathetic in her own way, but she was constitutionally unable to understand how Alex could be stupid enough to start a quarrel with Rod at exactly the moment he was being thrown together with an old love. It was hard for anyone to understand, especially for Alex, but after a while she managed to exonerate herself, at least in her own mind. It was a bit hard to do, but soon she had convinced herself that Rod was really the villain, that he had deliberately picked the fight with her so that he could guiltlessly take up again with Diana the next week.

In that state of mind Alex went home, without seeing Rod leave, without a word to him, certain as never before she'd never see him again. The trip had been a disaster, the summer was a shambles, and she was a wreck.

She got little sympathy from either Ellen or Miriam, not surprising in view of the fact that both of them got their version of the story from Cassie. Alex made a point of saying nothing. She threw herself into the work of the barn as never before. She had learned a lot already from showing alongside Rod and she didn't hesitate to put the knowledge to use. If it was what she would gain from the summer, so be it.

If Rod was missed by others—and he was—she refused to acknowledge that. She grew sharper and used an increasingly available supply of sarcasm to keep some of the older girls in line in Rod's absence. Two girls in particular, Andrea and Kathy, lead riders for Cassie's drill team, became abcessed thorns in Alex's side. Cassie managed them no better than did Alex, and she decided to dismiss them from the barn, regardless of how the move would upset Cassie's plans for the drill team, as soon as she found out for certain Rod wouldn't be back. He had always managed them easily, using both his quick wit and, undoubtedly, his sex appeal to keep them in order. If he returned, he was welcome to them, Alex thought, conscious of how much their cool arrogance reminded her of Diana Dunbar.

She had Rod's phone number to call if she needed to reach him, given before their quarrel (if that was what it had been), but she was determined nothing on earth would cause her to call him. That resolution was severely tested, however, when by the Wednesday of the second week one of the horses knocked down Alex's carefully built isolation ward and a whole lot more.

Ellen was parked in the open center of the barn near one of the box stalls directing several of the younger students as they went over the steps of grooming a horse. King Arthur was secured in cross ties as the girls worked on him. The path around King Arthur was blocked momentarily by some of the girls, so Ellen turned in her wheelchair just as another horse, Mannequin, appropriately nicknamed Dummy, was being brought through the barn for exercising. In the afternoon light the metallic flash of the wheelchair spooked Mannequin. He reared, his front hooves catching Ellen's chair either on the upswing or in coming down again, opinions differed on that point, tipping the chair over, wedging her against the side of the stall.

The chair itself protected her from the startled horse, which was brought under control, but Ellen was left unconscious, half in the chair, half on the floor. The girls, too young to know better, grabbed Ellen and held her in the wheelchair, still unconscious, as they tipped it back upright. One of the girls, now in full panic, began to push the chair on a dead run through the barn, heading for the house.

Alex and Cassie, who had rushed to the scene from outside, intervened in time to save Ellen from being pushed down the ramp and probably again being thrown from the chair. Cassie called an ambulance, but Ellen still had not revived by the time it arrived within minutes of being summoned. Alex rode with her to the hospital to explain what she knew of Ellen's normal condition as well as the accident.

Many anxious hours later Alex and Ellen's parents learned she was conscious and out of danger. The doctor, a young internist, told them it would be some time before they would be able to assess the effects of the accident on her disease. Because multiple sclerosis affects each victim differently, depending upon which nerve linings erode, and because each person's experience with the disease is subject to periodic—and largely unexplainable—attacks, countered by equally unpredictable times of remission, they and Ellen would have to wait and see.

It was not an easy prescription. Alex was wracked by guilt because she had exposed Ellen to danger. Mrs. Porter could hardly bring herself to look at Alex, so strong was her disapproval. But it was Ellen's father who broke Alex's heart. His grief was pure. He simply wanted his little girl to be whole.

Ellen had never told them she was teaching riding, or even that she went into the barn. She had known they would snatch her back to the stultifying safety of their devoted care, as Ellen always put it; "Back home to be shut away in the back bedroom." They were not unkind, but they refused to see that a life of watching TV with Mom and Dad was not enough for her.

Alex knew that Ellen, given the choice between safety and living life to the fullest, would always opt for challenge, regardless of the exposure to possible harm, but Alex's regrets were different. She didn't believe it had been wrong to have Ellen in the barn and around horses, but she knew she had been remiss in failing to teach the youngsters in Ellen's care basic livesaving techniques. They should have known not to move Ellen once she had fallen, and because they hadn't known better, Alex couldn't forgive herself.

It was Friday before anyone but the Porters could see Ellen. Alex did not wait alone, however. A steady stream of young and old riders accompanied Cassie, Gerald, and Miriam to the waiting room.

Wlen Alex took Ellen's thin hand in hers, Ellen asked, "Where's Rod?"

"In New York. It's Friday still."

"He'll be back."

Alex nodded, a lump in her throat.

"You don't believe me? I know."

Alex squeezed her hand. "Do you hurt?"

"Too much junk in me." Her eyes closed, then opened briefly. "Be okay. Promise."

Since the weekend show was local, Cassie and Alex took turns alternating between the show and the hospital watch. On Sunday evening it was Miriam with Alex in what they almost thought of as 'their' room, waiting for the Porters to leave Ellen so they could say good night. They had been there for over half an hour when Rod burst into the waiting room. He gave Miriam a taut smile and sat down on the couch opposite Alex.

"Why the hell did't you call me last Wednesday?" he demanded without preliminary.

"Wednesday?" Alex went stupid with shock.

"When Ellen was hurt. You had my number."

"I . . . lost it." She looked away. It wasn't true. The paper he'd written it on was in a zippered inner pocket of

154

her purse, dog-eared from the times she'd taken it out to call him, then chickened out.

"Don't give me that. You could have called Information. I wasn't in Africa, for God's sake."

Miriam spoke up. "Don't be too hard on her, Rod. She's stupid, but she means well."

He gave up glaring at Alex and looked at Miriam, addressing her in his normal tones. "How is she?"

"She's okay, getting there. She got a concussion and they're not too sure about her back. Getting hauled around like that may have caused more paralysis. They don't know how much is the accident and how much is just the disease kicking up again. The trauma of the accident may have started up another attack. They don't really know very much."

Miriam hitched herself on the plastic couch. Her feet didn't quite reach the floor, so the slippery material kept threatening to dump her off the couch. "Her parents are in there. Her mother isn't too happy about any of us. Can't say as I blame her."

Rod flicked a glance at Alex and got up to pace. Three times back and forth and·Ellen's parents emerged. Mrs. Porter headed immediately for the exit, but her father paused in the doorway to wish them good night. He looked at Rod questioningly, so Alex made the introduction without getting to her feet. He took Rod's outstretched hand. "She'll be happy to see you. She's been asking for you."

Rod looked back to Miriam, then went to see Ellen. Alex looked at the floor.

Miriam said, "You see? He came back. Now, why don't you smarten up and let him know how glad you are?"

Alex shifted in the chair. How could she be glad when

155

he was so miserable to her? She looked briefly at Miriam. "Maybe I'm just too stupid to be glad."

Miriam hooted to herself. After they sat several minutes in silence she got to her feet. "Let me drive myself back in your car. I'm too tired to wait my turn to see her. Just give her my love."

Alex bristled. She was not going to be a party to such a blatant attempt to throw her together with Rod. She turned away. "Not on your life. You can wait a few more minutes."

Rod came up behind Miriam. "You want a ride home, Miriam? I'm going now."

Miriam gave Alex a sorrowful smile and trotted off behind him, a squat figure taking three steps to his single loping stride. When they were gone Alex burst into tears of self-pity and anger. She hated them all. They were supposed to be *her* friends and not one of them was willing to see her side of anything having to do with their wonderful Rodney Gilbert. She was sniffling with abandon when a nurse paused between doors to ask, "Are you all right, miss?"

Alex straightened and came to her senses. "Yes. Sorry. I just got depressed."

"It happens. Your friend seems happier though. Why don't you see her a second. I think it will make you feel better."

She got up. "Thanks. I will." She gathered her pocketbook and the newspaper she'd brought but never looked at and went to Ellen's door.

Ellen did look better. She even laughed when she saw Alex's tear-streaked face. "See? I told you he'd come."

Alex nodded, lips trembling between a forced smile and more tears. "You look better. The nurse said."

"Nothing like a handsome man to perk me up. But you! Alex, you look terrible."

"Thanks," she half giggled, half sobbed.

"He's mad right now, but he'll get over it."

"I deserve it. I should have called him."

"No harm done."

"I wish I could believe that."

"You mean me or with Rod?"

"Both."

"I'm okay. More than okay. I'm going to be back soon, soon as I can. Rod said I have to come back because he's going to get me riding again. Can you believe it?"

Alex opened her eyes wide, startled beyond words.

"He said. He read about people with handicaps worse than mine who ride regularly. With some help of course, but they sit up there on a horse all by themselves and they ride." Ellen's eyes were shining. She pressed Alex's hand. "I'm going to do it, Alex. I really am."

"I believe you, honey. If anyone in the world can do it, you can."

"That's what Rod said." She sighed happily. "And *you* are going to end up as Mrs. Rodney Gilbert. That's the other part of my dream. I'm going to be your maid of honor, remember? I don't suppose I could ride the horse down the aisle, could I?"

Alex laughed. "You can ride anything you want, Ellen. Why not a horse?"

"That's what I think too." Ellen settled back dreamily. "So you go home and make up with Rod right away. Even if he's the one who's wrong."

Alex sighed. "How can I lose? I'm surrounded by such loyal support—for Rod, not me."

157

"We support you, don't worry. But you know how men are."

"No, I don't know how men are, Ellen. That's my problem. I seem to guess wrong every time. As Miriam puts it, I'm stupid."

"Never mind. You're learning. And Rod's only mad at you because he loves you and it scares him to death."

"If that's love, Ellen, I'm not sure I want it."

"Sure you do."

Alex kissed her and squeezed her hand. "I'm counting the days now till you get that first ride. Think about that now."

"I will. Good night."

Alex leaned against the closed door, eyes shut. Rod, oh, Rod. He was the best thing that ever happened to Ellen. For that alone she loved him.

Feeling happier than she had in weeks, Alex left the hospital determined to see Rod and apologize for not calling him. Whatever else might follow from that would depend totally on Rod, but she had been wrong and couldn't leave things this way any longer.

But Rod wasn't at the farm, and short of waiting in his room for him, she couldn't think what to do but to postpone her speech for another time—the first possible opportunity, she vowed.

The opportunity never seemed to arise, however. Rod was either absent or surrounded by others. He was polite to her in a particularly irritating way, as if he were laughing at her, as he probably was. Even Miriam, usually his staunch supporter, began to give him a sharp look now and then, and Cassie was plainly befuddled.

He spent his evenings away from the farm, but even Cassie didn't know where he went after he visited Ellen.

Ellen didn't know either, and although she wanted to promote Alex's cause with Rod, she was weak and sometimes unable to see anyone. So Alex never got to deliver her apology, and as the week wore on she was less and less inclined to seek the elusive opportunity.

If anything, Rod went out of his way to annoy Alex. He made decisions affecting the barn's operation that were plainly within Alex's dominion, something he had before been careful to avoid even the appearance of doing. They were not wrong decisions, but the wrong person was deciding. The tail was wagging the dog. It was her nightmare come true, but she didn't want to risk a confrontation with him so soon before their own horse show.

Their horse show, never before one of the major events in the local show season, was nevertheless always one of the principal money-making enterprises for the farm. This year, with Rod on hand, interest in the show was phenomenal. Alex had pulled out all the stops to try to make it the very best their modest facilities could produce. She had secured excellent judges and already the ground crews were beginning to upgrade the courses and groom every inch of the terrain. It was no time to rock the boat.

So Alex gritted her teeth and refused to give Rod the satisfaction of rising to his bait. She also went out of her way to back his authority, unnecessarily as far as others were concerned, but the charade was important to her own self-respect. She simply pretended before everyone else that she had conferred authority upon Rod, therefore what he did was with her blessing—a cowardly approach, she knew, but all she could come up with under pressure.

Whenever Alex felt depressed about her personal life, which happened more and more, she consoled herself by looking over the flood of entrants for their show. It put the

159

sparkle of dollar signs in her eyes, not as pleasant as the glow of love, perhaps, but Alex could live with that.

Cassie was handling registration for the show, a big job, but Alex always went over the tallies to keep abreast of the numbers, the better to make some crucial decisions. However much they had expanded their capacity, there was a definite limit to the number of both horses and people they could adequately service, and being greedy this once to take advantage of their momentary celebrity would only rebound to hurt them in the long run. People who pay entrance fees as high as what they were asking this year reasonably expect a smooth, organized show. To provide less would be to ruin themselves for future years, and Alex was not going to sacrifice Sunny Meadow Farm's reputation for a one-shot killing.

As she went over the numbers at her desk, Alex realized the cut-off point had been reached. But where to cut? Postmarks were the only fair criteria, so she began looking at the envelopes of the latest registrants. One name leaped at her from the paper—Diana Dunbar.

So even that wasn't over, she thought. Which presented a moral dilemma for Alex. She could pick a cut-off date that excluded Diana and perhaps no one would ever be the wiser. It was certainly what she ought to do, she knew. Why should she bend over backwards to allow a rival another crack at the man she loved? It would be stupid to allow Diana to compete here.

Alex looked at the date and time of posting. She added the numbers to see how many other entrants would be cut off along with Diana—only four. Not a critical number either way. Which made the decision harder to make. If by including Diana the number had been higher, it would have been a persuasive argument to exclude her. After all,

160

a dozen extra horses and riders would strain their capacity. But four? There would be that many, or more, who would be scratched at the last minute.

Cassie would call her all kinds of fool if she let Diana come, but as she stared at the registrations she knew she would do so. Otherwise how could she justify herself to Rod? Even if Cassie never found out, he would know. She would look like the stupid, jealous, possessive, though entirely without grounds, woman she felt herself to be.

She sighed and jumbled up the envelopes to look as if she had not sorted through them as she had. She then scribbled off a note to Cassie setting the cut-off date so that Diana was included and put it where Cassie would find it. Maybe she would get by without Cassie noticing either the name or what Alex had done. She laughed to herself. Sure, and soon pigs would fly!

But like her talk with Rod, the need to justify the cut-off date to Cassie never materialized. Alex's major moral victory over jealousy went unheralded as the week of the show edged nearer and nearer. In the rush of events tempers began to flare, briefly at first, but with growing intensity as the workload grew. Ellen's humor and knowing hand were sorely missed now.

Cassie kept Alex informed, more informed than she wanted, about every little tiff among the older girls, whose capacity for intrigue was, in Alex's opinion, positively Byzantine. Even though Kathy and Andrea were behind most of the problems, Alex was determined to leave them totally to Rod. He could dismiss them if he wanted to, but she would not. They were, after all, both excellent riders who paid their bills promptly.

Shortly before Alex intended to leave to visit Ellen, Cassie burst into her office, her blue eyes awash with tears.

She hurled herself into a chair and gave herself over to angry sobs.

"What's the matter, Cassie?" Alarmed, Alex went close and tried to put her arms around her friend.

Cassie pushed the chair back and looked up accusingly. "I know you're in love with him and you don't dare breathe near him, but you've got to stop him!"

Rod.

"What did he do, Cass?"

"He just can't do this to me! I've got that team going perfectly now, and it's taken all summer to teach those complicated maneuvers so they've got it down pat."

"I know, Cassie. You've done a fabulous job with the drill team. They're going to stop the show. What does Rod have to do with them?"

"If he has his way, they won't even get to perform. The whole thing will be ruined. All that work just wasted!"

Alex had to wait out another storm of tears before she got the answer to her question.

"I know they're horrible—just total brats—but Rod *can't* kick them out of the barn two weeks before the show. They're the drill team leaders, and no one else knows the routine the way they do. It'll be a disaster from start to finish without them!"

Kathy and Andrea. Alex looked into Cassie's distraught face and a red haze of rage blurred her vision. She whirled away from Cassie and flew down the stairs in search of Rod, no longer the least bit concerned about finding him alone. Every grievance against Rod, every slight to her authority, rose up like choking bile in her throat. Being a coward, avoiding confrontation, had bought her nothing, and she no longer cared who knew how she felt.

162

Naturally, now that she didn't care about talking to him privately, he was alone in the main barn for the first time in weeks.

"Rod, what the hell do you think you're doing?"

"Putting a saddle on F. T. here," he said mildly.

"Very funny. That's not what I mean and you know it. Just where do you get off sending Andrea and Kathy packing two weeks before the show, I'd like to know? You know perfectly well how important they are to the drill team."

"They can be replaced. It would be harder to replace the barn and all these horses."

"What are you talking about?"

He gave a furious yank on the girth before he turned the full force of his attention on Alex. "I suppose Cassie came crying to you and you never bothered to find out what they did, did you?"

He had her there. She looked at him blankly, knowing she was going to be caught in the wrong. Her anger had taken over and she'd never even asked Cassie why Rod dismissed them.

"I don't care what they did," she said defensively, blundering on to dig the hole a little deeper. "Whatever it was, it could have been smoothed over with a little tact, at least until the show is over."

"I thought you had at least one hard and fast rule here—that anyone who smoked in the barn was instantly dismissed. Or are the rules suspended until your precious show is over?"

She had to say something, so she asked, "Where were they smoking?" As if it made any difference! He was right and they both knew it. What's more, she couldn't question his right to dismiss them because even Steve had done it

163

in the past and she had backed him totally. It was the one unpardonable crime in a barn full of combustible hay and valuable horses.

Rod's look was scathing. "They were in the tack room and they wanted to get caught. They know my schedule as well as I do. If they hadn't been trying to force the issue, they would have picked another place. I could hardly ignore it either when three of the younger kids were right on my heels. It would have been the end of discipline around here."

There was absolutely nothing she could say. She had to apologize for her hasty misjudgment. She had to. But the words stuck in her throat. She looked down at her boots, trying to summon the apology, trying to force it past the angry lump in her throat. She opened her mouth and looked up into his triumphant brown eyes. Malicious enjoyment was written in every line of his face and Alex shut her mouth firmly. She'd fry in hell before she'd apologize with him looking like that!

"Sorry, boss lady," he said softly. "I know you're itching for a fight, but it looks like you'll have to pick on something else—like maybe what's really eating you."

His eyes held her pinned in place. She wanted to turn and run before he said another word, but her boots seemed to be nailed to the barn floorboards.

"We both know what's really bothering you, don't we?"

Alex whirled on her heel to make her escape, but she couldn't outrun his taunting words.

"You're frustrated, Alex. Just plain frustrated." He said it just loudly enough so she couldn't help hearing it, then his laugh chased her all the way down the wide ramp and out to the parking lot.

Arrogant, insufferable pig!

She slammed the car door and fumbled in her pocket for the keys. Anger made her clumsy and she stalled the car twice before she could get onto the road. All the way to the hospital Alex hurled epithets at Rod and his bloated male ego. Boss lady. How he loved to call her that at the precise times when he was in full control and she was in total disarray—and there were far too many times like that to suit Alex.

What bothered her more than his taunts, of course, was the fact that she had been completely wrong to go after him without all the facts. He had been right to dismiss the girls and he certainly had full authority to do so. Upset herself, Cassie had taken advantage of Alex's blindness, but it was the kind of emotionalism she should have dealt with handily. Except that her own emotions were even more out of control than Cassie's.

The drill team's loss of Andrea and Kathy wasn't even the tragedy Cassie pretended, Alex knew. The second in line could take over the leadership from the ousted girls without difficulty, especially with nearly two full weeks for rehearsals before the team's performance. With fourteen riders still involved, even the overall appearance of the matched pairs of riders carrying out dressagelike movements in patterns, all set to music, would not be adversely affected.

But it wasn't Cassie that Alex was mad at. It was herself. She owed Rod another apology, and no matter how his recent attitude had irritated her, she should have given it immediately. But she hadn't been able to do it, hadn't been able to shift emotional gears fast enough to suit him, and he'd taken advantage of her weakness to taunt her.

Damn him!

She jerked the car to a halt in the parking lot, so angry

that she charged unseeing past a startled Eliza Chandler on her way out the main hospital door as Alex entered.

"Alex?"

Alex whirled blindly on the figure calling her name, then laughed, self-conscious. "Eliza, I'm sorry. I didn't see you. How are you?"

"Fine, dear, just fine. You look lovely today. Are you going to see Ellen? I've just come and I must say she's doing well now again. Did you know she's going home tomorrow?"

"Home?" Alex was confused.

"She said her parents are going to take her home tomorrow. They have a therapist coming in every day for her, so she'll be able to keep up her progress. She has the most marvelous courage, doesn't she?"

"She certainly does." Alex was calming now. Of course the Porters would take Ellen home with them. The farm would be no place for her now, especially with the show coming up. Her only fear was that once they got her home with them they'd never agree to let her go again. And she wanted Ellen to be with them at the farm, not for her help at the barn, just for her company. With all her world in a shambles, Alex felt she needed Ellen, needed her courage.

Alex became aware of Eliza's appraising look, so she tried to pull herself together. "How was your vacation on the Cape?"

"Oh, lovely and restoring, as always. But how are you getting along, Alex? Under all that youthful beauty of yours, I think you look a bit tired."

"Things are a bit hectic just now. The show is only two weeks away, you know."

"I did know. In fact, I was going to call you to see if

you could come to dinner Saturday night this week. I know after this weekend it will be impossible for you, but Henry and I have a guest we'd love you to meet."

Alex laughed and so did Eliza, each knowing what those words meant.

"Actually, dear, this young man is something of an apology from Henry for getting you involved with Rod. I had grave misgivings about that, but Henry thought it would be marvelous. I do apologize for not being firmer. I knew he was something of a rake, and I should never have gone along with Henry. But you know how men can be." She smiled conspiratorially at Alex. "I really think Henry enjoys Rod's escapades vicariously." She tossed her silvery hair.

Alex couldn't seem to think of anything to say. She was getting tired of every woman in her acquaintance inviting her indulgence of men. Everyone else in the world, it seemed, knew "how men were" except herself.

"Do you know," Eliza went on confidentially, "when we got back from the Cape the neighbors came running to tell us all about his wild pool parties while we were gone? Evidently he had a regular parade of different girls there just about every night. Of course, Henry had told him to use the pool if he wanted, but I do think he could have used some discretion." She put her hand on Alex's arm. "Keep Saturday night open for us, dear. I'll call you. I *know* this man is much more suitable for you."

Alex turned away slowly as Eliza sketched a wave and went out into the sunshine. Her thoughts were a total jumble. Rod, Ellen, Rod again.

She walked the hospital corridor slowly, trying to piece together the information she'd received. So Rod had a whole series of pool parties, did he? Even allowing for some measure of exaggeration on the part of the neighbors, it meant she was not the only partner he had entertained. She knew he'd been there all night the night before she stayed with him, but somehow she'd assumed he had been alone. Why? she asked herself. Because Cassie didn't report back on him? She felt more than deflated. What had been a treasured memory was reduced to a shabby escapade, she herself just another notch in Rod's belt, a casual conquest.

At the same time, however, something in Alex rebelled at the way Eliza had assumed that Rod was just too much man for her to handle. It was what she had been telling herself ever since she first saw him, but to hear it from another person infuriated her, especially when it was laced with pity for her. Poor Alex, pretty enough, but she just can't cope with men.

Rod probably was a rake—whatever that antiquated word meant—but that didn't mean he couldn't change. She knew he was impossible. Hadn't she just seen him in action at his absolute worst? He was everything she'd been calling him on the way to the hospital—chauvinistic, macho, completely insufferable. But he was also the man who made her blood race, the man she loved, and she had absolutely no desire even to meet anyone Eliza would consider "suitable" for her.

But she would meet him, she decided, slowing down to gaze from one of the windows at the end of Ellen's corridor. And what's more, she intended to charm his socks off. Perhaps unwittingly, Eliza had again done Alex a favor, she decided. She had just presented her with a possible solution to her biggest problem with Rod. So far she had been the only one of them having to fight jealousy. He was pursued; she was not. Mr. Suitable would take care of that—perhaps.

If only he wasn't a wimp. She prayed the Chandlers wouldn't do that to her. If only he looked halfway decent, she could give Rod enough jealousy to give him heartburn.

That resolved, Alex steamed into Ellen's room.

"Wow," Ellen exclaimed. "Who lit a fire under you?"

She laughed. "The question should be 'Who are you going to light a fire under?' "

"Somehow I think I can guess—and it's about time, lady."

CHAPTER SEVEN

Alex came home from visiting Ellen at the hospital in a totally different frame of mind. She was completely unflappable, full of confidence. From the first she'd known she wanted to marry Rod, but she'd never dared acknowledge it, even to herself. It seemed too forward, too frightening. Something dark and superstitious inside her had believed it was asking for trouble, tempting fate, to acknowledge her desire. But denying it hadn't made it less her desire. All it had done was cripple her with a lot of false pretenses, made her seem too timid to be of interest to a man like Rod.

Her new attitude was immediately apparent to everyone, but she explained nothing. She tried not to be overbearing, however, and controlled her amusement when the others were puzzled, especially Rod. Although he tried to hide his reaction, she could see that his interest was piqued by the change in her. After all, their confrontation in the barn over Andrea and Kathy had sent her away near tears of rage and frustration; now to have her bounce back enough to issue a gracefully phrased and appropriate apology he accepted warily, well, there had to be an explanation. That's what his reason clearly told him, but he could find nothing handy that made sense of her new behavior.

For the rest of the week Alex rode a crest of good fortune. Her phone conversation with Eliza to set up her date was overheard by a reluctant Rod, enabling her to pretend for his benefit that Eliza was the stalwart George Babcock who was going to pick her up at seven the next day. She even blushed during her overheard chat, something Rod was sure to notice and that she could never have produced on demand except that what she was thinking about him easily brought the blood to her cheeks. Eliza had assured her that George Babcock was imminently presentable, tall and sandy-haired, very well dressed, and widely known in horse circles as a wealthy man with an appreciative eye for both horses and women. Henry had suggested the gold gown, but Alex had other plans, especially now that her tan was perfect.

It wasn't necessary to pretend excitement as Saturday evening drew near. Alex was beside herself wondering if Rod would be there to see her leave with George. She assured herself that even if he did leave before they did, he would hear about it, obliquely, perhaps, from Cassie and Miriam, and his own admittedly good imagination would do the rest of the work for her.

In a way she was amazed to find that Rod was still in the living room when she and George descended to leave. She decided he was too surprised to understand what she was doing. Certainly he had no idea how much he looked like her disapproving father as he looked over her dress, or he'd have gone anywhere just to keep her from seeing the wretchedness on his face. The dress was a slim fall of off-white silk. Like the gold gown, it was slit to the thigh on one side so she could walk. A cascade of soft pleats from one shoulder broke over her breasts and were recaptured at the waist to emphasize its slender span. She had purposefully worn her hair long and loose to torment him, and it was working, as anyone could see when Alex introduced George to all, including surly-looking Rod.

When she was tucked into George's Mercedes she looked back at the house and saw a light go on in Rod's room. Then she turned to look at George for the first time, aware that she was probably not being fair to this attractive man. He was exactly what Eliza had promised— pleasant, suitable, no one to put stars in her eyes, but exactly the kind of man everyone would choose for her, and decidedly no wimp. In fact, Rod would probably be particularly vulnerable to jealousy over someone like George because he had the social and economic advantages Rod lacked. George was the kind of man Diana Dunbar had deserted him to seek, so he would find it easy to believe that Alex wanted the same thing. And for a while, for as long as it took, she intended to reinforce his suspicions.

The evening and the devoted attention of George Babcock also worked as a balm on Alex's somewhat shredded ego. George gave every indication of being genuinely fascinated by her, both personally and as a woman running a horse farm. Before the evening was over he declared that he would stay another week in order to attend the Sunny Meadow horse show. Eliza and Henry took on the prideful glow of those who believe themselves successful matchmakers, and they urged him to remain with them.

Before he started the car to drive Alex home, George took out a pipe and started to fill the bowl just as he remembered to ask, "Do you mind if I smoke?"

Alex breathed the pipe tobacco fragrance deeply. "Now I know you're a real lawyer. My father smoked the same tobacco, and I haven't smelled it in years. I'm probably going to cry," she admitted, trying to laugh instead.

George stopped loading the pipe, uncertain what to do. Alex touched his arm, "No, no. Go ahead. It's just a momentary thing. That particular odor is emotionally loaded for me, but I'm really not going to dissolve on you."

"It would be all right if you did." He puffed to start the pipe, looking over the flaring bowl at her. "I can think of things a lot worse than comforting a beautiful woman like you." He snapped his lighter away and continued looking at her, frowning. "Do you mind if I ask you a question?"

"You can always ask and if I choose, I can always not answer."

"I just wondered what your relationship is with Rod Gilbert."

"Do you know Rod?"

"By reputation. Surprisingly, we've never met before."

"And what is his reputation? With you?" Alex parried.

"Excellent trainer, gets superb results. Personally, rather stubborn and hardheaded. With an eye for attractive women."

"I don't think I'd argue with much of that assessment," Alex said. "Like anyone who's successful in a crowded field, he has developed ways of dealing with those around him and he tends to keep to those ways. Why not? They work for him."

"You haven't answered the question. I guess you choose not to."

"I wondered why you asked."

"Just a feeling I picked up on when we were introduced, an undercurrent, shall we say, of something possessive on his part." If George had not been the burly and attractive man that he was, his expression would have looked positively coy to Alex.

She laughed. "If you know Rod's reputation with women, what makes you think he doesn't know yours?"

He nodded and smiled around the pipe stem. "Touché."

As George drove her home, Alex mulled over the pros and cons of letting him come up to her living room. If Rod was there, she definitely would, but if he wasn't . . . She still hadn't decided by the time they pulled into the driveway and she discovered Rod's car was gone. At the door she paused and turned to George. "Would you like to come up for a quick drink? I don't think it's too late."

Their conversation was relaxed and pleasant as Alex's new confidence held up under circumstances that, before Rod, she would have found daunting. She compared George constantly with Rod, her prototype of what a man should be. He was cool where Rod was passionate, even in matters of opinion; affable rather than funny; and his way of moving was lazy, giving the impression of unhurried ease. Without the sense of tightly coiled tension ready to erupt any second, George seemed less dangerous than Rod, so that Alex dropped her guard a bit too much.

She had kicked off her shoes and curled her feet under her on the couch so that when George kissed her their heads were nearly even. His kiss was not unpleasant, just so very different from Rod's as to not seem at all what a kiss should be. He had no moustache, for one thing, and there was no tension in his lips or in his arms as they were around her. He did not seem to have anything else in mind but to give her a long slow kiss, very peaceful, very boring. She made sure she seemed to be kissing him back before she drew away. "George, I think you should be going now. I have an early day tomorrow and a busy week."

"Okay," he said, kissing her again. "But not until you say you'll have dinner with me tomorrow."

"I'm not sure I can."

"You have to eat anyway. At your convenience. I'll call you around one o'clock."

"All right. That's very nice of you." She took his hand as he helped her to her feet. She didn't put her shoes back on as she stood at the door with him. Before he shut the door behind him he drew her against him, kissing her yet again with the same slow thoroughness. She said good night and went back inside.

Without touching the curtain she looked over the moonlit front yard. Rod's little Audi was there, parked by the barn rather than near the house, where George was getting into his car. So he had come back in time to find out that George had been upstairs with her. She couldn't keep from smiling, wondering how he felt. She hoped jealousy was eating into him as it had into her for the past few weeks. She was sure it was, otherwise why would George have noticed that "something possessive" on his part?

Alex knew jealousy was a base emotion. She hadn't enjoyed one moment of it, and it was not an emotion she wanted Rod to feel very long. But he was so cocky, so sure of himself, so sure of her. He had to be rocked out of that complacency. He had to start worrying about whether someone else might steal her away. He was possessive about her in an abstracted, almost casual way. Good old Alex. In love with him. A bit of a pest about it all besides.

She hoped tonight had made him look at her again— look at her on rich George Babcock's arm, in his car, and, yes, maybe even in his bed. She wouldn't do that, but she very much wanted Rod to be aware that it could happen. She wanted him to think about how he would feel about that possibility. She hoped it was on his mind right now.

The only disquieting note in Alex's thoughts was a question: How could she be sure the game she was playing would end the way she wanted it to? Now that Rod was perhaps worrying about another man in her life, when and how should she let him know it wasn't real?

Before she realized what she was doing she opened the door and padded down, heading for the kitchen and a glass of milk. What could be wrong with getting a glass of milk? There was a crack of light under Rod's door, so on the way to the kitchen she walked to it and tapped. When he opened the door she realized her mistake. His shirt was untucked and unbuttoned, his chest mostly bare and dark with hair at the level of her eyes. He leaned against the doorframe, looking down at her without a word. Her mouth went dry and she stepped back. How could she have forgotten the way his closeness affected her?

"I just came down for a glass of milk and I saw your light. Would you care to join me?" Amazingly, her voice didn't quaver, but it took all her dwindling reserves of confidence to stand there waiting for him to answer. His face was deeply shadowed, but hers was not. A shaft of light from behind him fell directly onto her face and gown, making it easy for him to read her tremulous anxiety.

"A glass of milk?" He opened the door wider but still

slouched arrogantly against the door. She could hear the bemused smile in his voice and her memory reconstructed his expression without needing to see him. "How about a can of beer instead?" He stepped back.

She lingered and he reached for her arm to draw her into the room. "I have beer here. Or don't you drink beer dressed like that?"

"I'll have a beer." She looked around as he went to a small refrigerator and got out two cans. The room was a mess. There was even a saddle on the floor by the couch. He tossed some clothes from the couch onto the saddle and gestured for her to sit. He removed a towel so he could sit beside her before he popped the cans open and handed one to her.

"So how was your evening?" He sat back, crossing a knee with a booted foot.

She took a drink. "Fine."

"Eliza and Henry?"

"Fine." She drank again, awkwardness overcoming her by leaps and bounds. He just looked at her as she kept sipping the unwanted beer. Finally she could stand it no longer. "Look, I'm sorry. This wasn't a very good idea. You were going to bed." She inched forward on the lumpy couch to get up, abandoning her beer on the flat wooden arm of the couch.

"That doesn't matter," he drawled, "unless you wanted to join me."

She got up, but so did he, looming over her, an obstacle between her and the door.

"Why did you come here, Alex?"

She licked her dry lips. "It . . . was just an impulse. I told you . . ."

"You were getting a glass of milk," he finished for her. "Other than that."

She stepped back, the wrong direction, when, short of achieving her wish that the floor would open and swallow her whole, she wanted to be safely out of this room again. "I don't know, Rod. We haven't been on very good terms lately and I just wanted to . . ." She couldn't think how to go on.

"Wanted to what?" he challenged her, not giving her an inch. "Wanted to show me your gown? Wanted to tease me? Was that it? It wasn't enough for you to send George Babcock home with steam coming out his ears, you wanted to see if you could still get a rise out of me as well."

She put her hands to her ears, as if trying to block his soft, mocking voice. "Rod, don't." She was going to cry. "I'm sorry, I didn't think."

"That excuse is getting old, Alex."

He was doing it again, she realized. He was intimidating her with his size and his control. She took her hands down from her head and straightened to stand as tall as she could in stocking feet, summoning back the invincible feeling she'd brought home from the hospital.

Renewed, she took a deep breath and gave him back the challenging look he was giving her. She put one hand on her hip and stuck out her chin.

"So tell me, *can* I still get a rise out of you? Or do I have to settle for George Babcock's steaming ears?"

His reaction was all she could have desired; a whistle of air as he caught his breath, a small dry chuckle, and a kiss that crushed her light dress against the furry warmth of his chest. He held her by one hand spread warmly over her lower back, the cold can of beer heedlessly pressing higher on her back as he made no secret of his excitement. When his hands traveled up her back so that the can touched her bare skin she yelped and he let her go.

"Go upstairs," he ordered. "I'll be right up." He caught her arm as she turned away, her head spinning. "Don't take off that dress. I want to do that."

She had no memory of walking upstairs, only of once again being back in her living room. Somehow her attention fell on George's glass on the coffee table and it seemed urgent to be rid of that glass and her own beside it. She carried them to the bathroom. She was back pacing the living room when he came inside and shut the door, looking for her first in the bedroom, although the table lamp beside the couch was on. He stopped by the doorway.

"I just said don't undress. I didn't mean you had to hide."

She tried a smile as he walked slowly closer.

"Teasing again?" She shook her head. "Shy again?" She nodded. "I still can't believe you knocked on my door."

"Neither can I. But I'm glad I did." He was close but still not touching her.

"Sometimes I think there are two of you. One is a trembling rabbit with big round eyes—like now—and the other is, I don't know, I was going to say bold as paint, but that isn't quite it. But it's the one we've been seeing lately, the one who knocked poor George on his ear, the one who knocked on my door."

"Why do you call him poor George?"

"Because he still doesn't know what hit him. He almost fell down the stairs tonight. What did you do to him?"

She smiled. "Wouldn't you like to know?"

His smile grew strained. "I'm sure I do know. The truth is you probably didn't do a damn thing but sit there looking pure and sweet, just letting that dress do all the work for you."

"You sound as if I should have helped the dress along."

His laugh was harsh, but hers bubbled up delightedly.

"You sound positively jealous, Rod."

"Surprise, surprise."

She put her arms up to his shoulders. "Stop looking so fierce and kiss me."

He didn't unbend. "That's what was supposed to happen, wasn't it? All this tonight was cooked up to make me jealous."

"Cooked up?" Alex took her arms down. "Nothing was cooked up. George was imported to meet me—Eliza and Henry at work again—but other than that, it's all absolutely straight, and I had nothing to do with that. I had a perfectly respectable, enjoyable evening with an attractive man who seemed to find me attractive."

"Are you going out with him again?"

"Yes."

"When?"

"Tomorrow."

"When is he leaving?"

"I don't know. He decided tonight to stay for the show."

"I bet he did."

"Well, why not? You have Diana to amuse yourself with, why shouldn't I have someone?"

"Dear God. Diana. Do you have to keep bringing her up?"

"I'm not bringing her up. She's bringing herself up."

"What are you saying?"

"Don't pretend after spending two weeks with her you don't know about her coming to the show."

"To our show?"

"What else?"

"I didn't know that."

"Well, now you do, so just lay off about George."

"You just don't know what you're getting into with him."

"You know, that's really funny. He was trying to warn me about you."

He turned away with a soft curse and Alex walked to the couch to sit on the arm, watching him tiredly. In spite of all the magnetism between them they had managed once again to face off, locked in another stupid quarrel when they should have been loving.

"Do you love Diana?"

"No."

"When you were just there did you sleep with her?"

"No."

"Why not?"

"Alex, I don't think that's—"

She got up and walked toward him. "It matters to me. I may not have a shred of pride to be saying this, but I don't care. I think you care about me. You know I care about you, but if that doesn't matter to you, then I'm not going to let it matter to me. I'm not going to hold my breath waiting for you to wake up and smell the roses."

His fists were clenched on his hips. "I don't like ultimatums, Alex, and that's what that sounds like."

"Too bad what you don't like." She put her hand flat on his bare chest. "I'm sure there are as many things you don't like as there are that I don't like." She moved her hand up toward his neck. "So tell me why you rejected Diana." She went closer to him. "And don't try to tell me she didn't want you back."

181

"I don't know what she wanted. I didn't care."

"Because of me?"

"Alex, for God's sake!"

"I have to know. Don't be so old-fashioned, Rod. You can tell me why. Either it had something to do with me or it didn't. I can take it either way."

"She didn't appeal to me."

"Why not?" Alex was close to kissing him.

"I don't know. She was just too forward, too calculating."

"Like I'm being now?" She had no idea where her bravado was coming from.

He took her shoulders, sighing. "As a matter of fact, you're about five times worse right now than she ever was."

Alex smiled. "Good." She kissed him softly, a light brush of her lips that he didn't let end with that. His hands on her shoulders were warm, almost rough, but she drew back. "But even if I'm worse I appeal to you?"

He looked exasperated. "Will you shut up, please."

"Not until you tell me how you feel about me."

"Right now I feel like throttling you."

She was relentless. "Besides that." She hung from his shoulders. "Have you ever told a woman you loved her?"

"No."

"But you love me."

He laughed. "Do I?" In spite of himself he was amused.

She nodded against his shoulder. "You have to. Or like poor George Babcock you'll be falling down those stairs in a few minutes. All by yourself."

"You know a man never means what he says when he's being coerced this way, don't you?"

"I don't care if you mean it or not. I just want you to

182

practice saying the words." A small part of herself, a very small part, was shocked that what she said was true. She didn't care. She looked into his glaring eyes.

"Okay, Alex, I love you. Now are you happy?"

She frowned, thinking. "Maybe if I heard it again . . ."

His hands tightened on her waist. "Damn it, Alex . . ."

She threw herself against him. "I'm happy. I'm happy. No one's called me Damn It Alex for so long." She hugged him as hard as she could, stretching up to his mouth. "Oh, Rod, I missed you."

"I missed you too. God, I missed you." He kissed her neck, her ears, her eyes, and finally her yielding mouth. When she let him talk again his voice was thick. "You know, I was mad at you for not telling me about Ellen because I wanted an excuse to come back early."

"You would have come back early?"

"If you'd called. I was looking for an excuse." He sighed. "You were right about the deal Ed Dunbar cooked up. He didn't really need me. It was for Diana. But after one conversation that was over."

"One conversation?"

"Yeah."

"I'd love to have heard it."

"No, you wouldn't."

"She loved you?"

"No. She just wanted back what got away. Love isn't a big part of Diana. With her it's just want."

"That's what you told me at first." She giggled. "And at second."

"Well, love is scary. I didn't think I could stand being loved the way you went at it. I was used to a simpler

183

relationship. You kept looking at me with those frightened eyes and it seemed to be too much. But when I saw Diana I knew it was just the look I needed to see. I was like a horse to her, a good prospect that got away and she wanted it back. Then I couldn't wait to get back here to you."

"Then why were you so awful to me when you got back?"

"I don't know. I'm not used to feeling like this."

She leaned back. "Like what?"

"I don't know."

She gave him her schoolteacher stare.

"Alex, I'm not going to change overnight. Words aren't my thing."

"Oh, yeah? It seems to me I've heard some pretty eloquent words from you in the cause of seduction."

He laughed. "Well, I learned to do that over a lot of years."

"I'm not going to wait a lot of years for you to work up a new routine."

"Boss lady, you are getting to sound like a very bossy lady." He kissed her, holding her firmly. "I think it's time I put you in your place."

Before she could say a word he picked her up and carried her to her bedroom. He sat on the edge of the bed, holding her on his lap briefly before he lowered her back onto the bed and leaned over her.

"When I saw you come downstairs dressed like this tonight, I just about went out of my mind. I wanted to knock Babcock into next week and haul you back up here so fast it would make your head swim. I swear I just wanted to chase you all the way up the stairs and lock you in your room."

"You looked just like my father would have looked."

Rod laughed. "It wasn't all that fatherly. I wanted to lock myself in here with you."

Alex pulled his head down, offering her mouth to be kissed. When she reached inside his mouth with the tip of her tongue he pulled her hard against him, rolling over so she was on top of him. With one hand he took her hair, his fingers weaving into the long strands, holding her head.

"How does the dress unfasten?"

She started to rise to find the hooks, but he held her fast.

"Tell me with words, schoolteacher."

"After you tell me some words."

"Please? Thank you?" His fingers tightened on her hair, so she could barely shake her head. "I love you," he said into her ear, tracing the edge of her lobe with his tongue. She collapsed against him. "The dress, damn it."

"Hooks and eyes on the shoulder. You'll need two hands."

"I'll manage."

After a long breathless struggle he did manage, but the top merely folded down to look like a strapless gown. "You'll have to let me go." He did and she sat up to reach under her gown and remove her panty hose.

He watched, leaning on one elbow, touching her breast through the cloth, tracing the nipple with one finger. "I knew you didn't have on a bra," he accused.

"It's built in, sort of." She moved toward him and lifted her hair from her back. "More hooks," she directed. He released them and the gown fell open. She turned and lifted her arms for him to take it off over her head. He shrugged off his shirt and put the dress aside before he took her, kneeling, into his arms. She undid his belt and

185

zipper until, with a strangled sound, he turned away to take off the rest of his clothes.

When he came to lie beside her his eyes were dark with passion. "You know you're not going anywhere with Babcock tomorrow, don't you?"

"Today, you mean."

"Ever, I mean."

"Why not?"

"Because I won't let you." He leaned on one arm over her.

She put her arms around his shoulders. "It will take more than a couple of 'I love you's' to stop me."

"How many?"

"It's hard to put a number on something like that. You see, George is a good marriage prospect."

"And I'm not?"

She gave him a thoughtful look. "I don't know. I think you like your freedom, answering to nobody, a girl in every town."

"That gets old."

"Does it? Maybe I'd like to try it and see."

"I thought you wanted to get married a second ago."

"How can I talk to you if you're going to keep track of every little thing I say and use it against me?"

"You mean I could tell you I'll marry you and you might not be listening?"

"I'm listening. But you don't *tell* a woman you'll marry her, you *ask* her if she'll marry you."

He buried his head in her neck and kissed down to her breasts, saying something she couldn't hear. She got her fingers into his thick hair and tried to pull his head up. "What did you say?"

He let go of her and laughed. "Picky, picky, picky."

Alex started to laugh too until he began touching her in earnest, and then she clung to him, giving herself up entirely to his loving. She strained to put every inch of her body into contact with him, trying to surround him, to hold him, with her blind need.

The knowledge that he loved her was like champagne in her blood. She felt she would float off into space if it had not been for his arms about her and the thrilling weight of his body pressing her against the bed. A primitive sense of belonging to Rod coursed through her veins, making her pliant and liquid.

His body was all tensile strength, lean and corded with muscles, but it was his face Alex would never tire of watching. Every thought he had registered there instantly, one expression chasing the other nimbly over his mobile features. No one she had ever known could go so quickly from irritation to amusement to passion.

She let her hands roam over his neck, shoulders, and arms, eagerly offering her mouth to his kiss. "You were right about me," she sighed beside his moustache. "I was frustrated."

"I knew because I was playing pot to your kettle." His smiling mouth outlined her lips with nibbling kisses that made her try to pull him closer. His kiss was first sweet, then passionate as she opened to him, drawing his tongue to deeper, more complete forays in imitation of their ultimate union. His mouth left hers only to make adoring circuits of her breasts. "You're so lovely," he breathed, watching as her nipple pebbled responsively.

"Oh, Rod, please," she whimpered, arching toward him. "I need you so."

Then, as if those were the exact words he required from her, he slowly merged with her, married his hardness to

187

her soft warmth in a moment of protracted bliss. "I love you, Alex. Oh, how I love you." His arms were like a vise around her, holding her, filling her with his love. She didn't move, didn't breathe, while every fiber of her body absorbed his imprint, gathering strength to respond to the glory of this moment out of time.

She answered each drive of his hips, matching his ardor with her own hunger. The world existed only through each other, but because it was a world of tenderness as well as of passion, of giving as well as of taking, it was a long time before Alex could bring herself to whisper, "That's three and four."

Rod fell away from her, spent. She saw the flicker of puzzlement before he rolled to his side with a laugh. He tucked her under his arm. She curled into him and he blew her hair from his face. "You talk too much."

He ran the palm of his hand down her arm from her shoulder and pulled her closer, putting one leg over her legs like a claim. "Alex, marry me."

She turned her head to the side, her breath shallow. "Do you mean that?"

"Why wouldn't I?"

"You're not just teasing me?"

He propped up onto his elbow and smoothed the hair back from her face. "No. God knows I love to tease you, in every way, and I suppose that's part of why I haven't asked before. But you're what I want, what I have wanted for a long time."

"For how long?" She turned to see his face.

"You were right about Diana. I couldn't be sure until I saw her again. I'd been so used to thinking of her the way I wanted her to be I wasn't sure of my judgment. But it was strange when I went back. I was a different person.

188

She was the same, but I'd changed and I just kept wanting you."

"I love you, Rod. I don't know when I knew I wanted to be your wife, but I didn't admit it to myself until Eliza told me you'd had other women at their house."

"But I didn't. Just you. And you and Ellen earlier. I was alone the night before."

"That's crazy. Are you sure?"

"Of course I'm sure."

"The neighbors told her you'd had wild pool parties."

"That was you. Or have you forgotten?"

"They must have thought I was two different people. I had on different suits and my hair was different."

"So you can explain to Eliza that you were the naked girl in the pool."

"Oh, no." Alex laughed. "Well, at least it blasted me out of my cocoon and made me take the chance with George."

"No more George."

"No more George, love. He never was anyway." Alex kissed his scratchy chin, sitting up. "Then where did you go these last few evenings if there was no other woman?"

"I was getting riding lessons."

"Riding lessons? You?"

"For Ellen. There's a woman I'd heard of who helps handicapped riders and she's been showing me what to do. I also went to see Ellen and arranged for her to come back after the show so we can start."

"Can she do it so soon?"

"Her therapist is all for it. She's doing some extra exercises. She can do it."

"You know, even when I hated you I still loved you because of Ellen."

Rod pulled her back into his arms, molding her to his body. "Yeah? Well, then, after I get Ellen going again, maybe I'll take you on as a project. If you're going to be my wife, you're going to have to learn to ride the Gilbert way."

His kiss stopped her indignant explosion, turning it to helpless laughter as he muttered into her neck. "I know some very effective exercises."

LOOK FOR NEXT MONTH'S
CANDLELIGHT ECSTASY ROMANCES ®

210 LOVERS' KNOT, *Hayton Monteith*
211 TENDER JOURNEY, *Margaret Dobson*
212 ALL OUR TOMORROWS, *Lori Herter*
213 LOVER IN DISGUISE, *Gwen Fairfax*
214 TENDER DECEPTION, *Heather Graham*
215 MIDNIGHT MAGIC, *Barbara Andrews*
216 WINDS OF HEAVEN, *Karen Whittenburg*
217 ALL OR NOTHING, *Lori Copeland*

Candlelight

Ecstasy Romances™

- [ ] 209 **DESIRABLE COMPROMISE,**
  Suzanne Sherrill......   11903-0-14
- [ ] 208 **PLAY TO WIN,** Shirley Hart 16939-9-11
- [ ] 207 **BRISTOL'S LAW,** Rose Marie Ferris.............10803-9-66
- [ ] 206 **THE MAN WHO CAME TO STAY,**
  Margot Prince....   15298-4-18
- [ ] 205 **DANCE FOR TWO,** Kit Daley.......................11662-7-15
- [ ] 204 **AFTER THE LOVING,** Samantha Scott..........10050-X-33
- [ ] 203 **A CHARMING STRATEGY,** Cathie Linz.........11177-3-21
- [ ] 202 **REACH FOR THE STARS,** Sara Jennings......17241-1-53
- [ ] 201 **DARING PROPOSAL,** Tate McKenna 11657-0-20
- [ ] 200 **MIDNIGHT MEMORIES,** Emily Elliott 15614-9-23
- [ ] 199 **SENSUOUS PERSUASION,** Eleanor Woods..17954-8-19
- [ ] 198 **DOUBLE PLAY,** Natalie Stone 12119-1-12
- [ ] 197 **DESIGN FOR DESIRE,** Anna Hudson 11848-4-20
- [ ] 196 **GUARDIAN ANGEL,** Linda Randall Wisdom ..13274-6-11
- [ ] 195 **RELUCTANT MERGER,** Alexis Hill Jordan......17375-2-10
- [ ] 194 **A LASTING IMAGE,** Julia Howard.................14723-9-16

$1.95 each

At your local bookstore or use this handy coupon for ordering:

DELL BOOKS   B084A
P.O. BOX 1000, PINE BROOK, N.J. 07058-1000

Please send me the books I have checked above. I am enclosing $ _____ (please add 75c per copy to cover postage and handling). Send check or money order—no cash or C.O.D.'s. Please allow up to 8 weeks for shipment.

Name _____

Address _____

City _____ State / Zip _____